RECKONING

— at the —

RIVIERA
ROYALE

THE FIFTH ANTY BOISJOLY MYSTERY

RECKONING AT THE RIVIERA ROYALE

1   Back at Bat at Baccarat..1

2   Sycophants, Unknown Aunts,
    and a Sudden Glance at Chance Romance..........................13

3   The Relevance of the Evidence
    of the Reticence of Elephants....................................24

4   A Yacht Fraught with Lots of Plots................................33

5   The Bolder the Yodeller the Colder the Shoulder.................43

6   The Clown Found Ground
    and Renowned as an All-Round Hound...............................53

7   Baffling Business on the Bustling Bow.............................62

8   The Chaotic Continuity of the Croupier Community............71

9   The Stagey Cryptic of the Cagey Critic............................80

10 The Net Sum of Jetsam...91

11 Rigging Roulette at the Riviera Royale...........................99

12 Anty's Aunty Raises the Ante....................................108

13 The Flume and Form of the Looming Storm.......................120

14 The Abominable Facts of All Animal Acts........................127

15 The Multitude of Motives
    for the Mystifying Murder of Max Minefield.....................138

16 Dread, Dismay and Danger,
    and a Banana-Coloured Blazer...................................148

17 A Swindle of a Scam of a Flimfam of a Sham....................158

18 A Menacing Beckoning to an Unsettling Reckoning............169

19 Reckoning at the Riviera Royale.................................180

20 Reconciliation at the Riviera Royale............................186

    Anty Boisjoly Mysteries...195

CHAPTER ONE

Back at Bat at Baccarat

IT HAD BEEN A LITTLE OVER A YEAR since I'd seen my mother and, I assumed at the time, slightly longer since she'd last committed murder. When I arrived at the Riviera Royale, however, another death had already occurred.

I may be giving the retelling more latitude than I ought, at this point, because initially nobody considered it a very suspicious death. Peculiar, certainly, but not very suspicious. So I'll jog back a bit and start with the receipt of a letter from my mother, inviting me to join her on the *Cote d'Azur*.

I confess I wasn't particularly anxious to see Mama, who had clippered off for the south of France the very evening of my father's final leaving do, but I felt it was time for a reckoning of the dodgy nature of his passing. What's more, her letter was so drippingly sentimental that I was left with little choice:

'*Do come. Weather divine.*'

Practically tear-soaked, by my mother's standards. I arranged passage at once.

Cap Royale is an orphaned little rock in the French Riviera. Not a cape at all, any longer, but an awkward accidental island that one accesses first by train to Portsmouth, steamer to Nice, then train again along the coast, then a jolly oscillation over curmudgeonly currents and visible reefs in a leaky skiff.

The island isn't far from the coast and in fact was walking

1

distance at some point in the past before a natural causeway was deliberately collapsed by developers who believed that, firstly, it would increase the exclusivity of the destination and that, secondly, this was desirable. They were bang-on about that first thing. The causeway, as was explained to me during the crossing by Pilque, the withered, weathered, wizened skipper of *le fiable,* had served as a natural breakwater, and now the tides take their vengeance in the form of a unidirectional whirlpool with the island at the centre. The effect on marine traffic is an orbital trajectory to the marina from shore, the long way round the island, carried by the current with little effort on the part of Pilque, who was hence freed to tell me all this.

So we took a leisurely tour around the island, Pilque, my valet Vickers, and myself. On the west side, which glowed orange in the face of the setting sun, was a cosy cove of a stony beach at the bottom of a high cliff. At the top of the cliff was a spindly copse of waving palm trees and at the bottom, on the beach, were immense, red and white striped tents. Pilque was unable to explain the tents, but he speculated, somewhat mystifyingly at the time, that this was probably where they kept the elephant.

On the point — the bit of Cap Royale which faces the infinite horizon — the geography is friendlier and greener, and it rolls gently from a high plateau to a coastline of calanques and clear waters. At the top is the Riviera Royale, an ornate, Victorian-era hotel and casino built to attract and amuse those whose delicate consciousness of class cannot abide the prattling proletariat gathered round the gaming tables of Monte Carlo or desperately huddling their yachts into the deepwater ports of Saint Tropez.

It didn't work out as planned. The Riviera Royale commands a majestic view of the aptly named *Cote d'Azur,* the grounds are a tropical Eden of palms and pines and cactus and vines, and the hotel itself is a lavish, luxurious, baroque and balconied billet fit for the queen for whom it was built. But there are no queens nor kings. Not even any nobility to speak of, so far as I understand, and that was rather the whole point of the exercise.

Sometime in the roaring 1880s — this was after the area had been ceded to the French by Italy — Queen Victoria and her considerable entourage began wintering on the Riviera. This brought a tremendous trade in followers of imperial fashion, and one enterprising and ambitious property developer gambled that if he could tempt Victoria to settle on one luxurious destination, custom-built to flatter and charm the grandmother of Europe, with faithful and flawless reproductions of British custom and cuisine, such a destination couldn't fail to be a goldmine.

The turning point, which came soon after the grand opening, was literal. HMS *Victoria and Albert,* on its first inspection tour of the island, got caught in the whirlpool, was very nearly scuttled on the reef, turned on its heel and steamed back to Nice. Legend has it Vicky never even glanced up from her knitting.

Now, in the sunny southern spring of 1929, the hotel had found its level as long-term storage for Britain's untethered itinerants, such as the dowager Boisjoly.

As we twirled helplessly around the point, a steam yacht, moored a safe distance from shore, came into view, followed by the shallow marina where sleeping sailboats swooned slowly in the glistening waves. Pilque put us ashore with our trunks and we were committed.

The lobby of the Riviera Royale was belle epoque dazzle — all fiddly fixtures and furnishings, copper wallpaper, marble floors in floral motif, billowy, gauzy drapery, and an immense skylight of marine blue that gave the foyer a mystical, submerged hue, like one of the nicer hotels in downtown Atlantis.

"Monsieur Boisjoly." A prim, pressed, penguin of a chap struggled out from behind the reception rampart and bore down upon us in an obsequious quickstep. He had a topiaried moustache and was short and round and wound up with the electric energy of the professionally affable. He was meticulously brocaded in a manner that paired perfectly with the lobby.

That he recognised me was no surprise — doubtless he'd been told to expect a tall, slim, chestnut-haired Englishman in his late twenties and his valet, Vickers, gentleman's gentleman and family heirloom, who was old when the Riviera Royale was merely a bad idea. What was unexpected, but shouldn't have been, was the ironically incorrect pronunciation of the family affliction — 'Boisjoly' is correctly pronounced 'Beaujolais', like the wine region, and meets with all manner of abuse back home, but here in France, the land of its birth, it was now reduced to its 'bwah-jolie' origins.

"Beaujolais," I gently corrected. "Like the wine region."

"Yes," said the penguin. "Rémy Beaujolais, at your service, Monsieur Bwah-jolie."

"Not really."

"I you assure." Rémy Beaujolais put his hand on his heart.

"Right oh, well, this is novel," I said. "Perhaps we'd best skip straight to Anthony, Rémy, if I may call you Rémy."

"Bien sur." Rémy bowed into the privilege.

"Anty, actually, to my global network of intimates."

"Anty." Rémy smiled broadly and shook my hand. "Your mother could not welcome you herself, Anty…"

"She's at the casino," I concluded for him.

"She is." Rémy brightened. "How for you know this?"

"Because there's a casino."

"She did not wish to pose you the rabbit," Rémy assured me. "This is the expression in English, yes?"

"If it's not, Rémy, it should be. I'll take it up at the next meeting."

"You are most kind."

I left Rémy to organise the fetching of the trunks from the dock and Vickers to supervise their allocation to our respective rooms, while I inspected my rambling royal suite and its two balconies, salon, boudoir, and glittering bathroom complete with claw-footed tub the size of a fishing boat. It was here I awaited Vickers and something formal and white with brass buttons, suitable for braving the female Boisjoly in her natural habitat.

Mother was *banque* at baccarat. This placed her at the centre of a kidney-shaped table in the centre of the opulent casino hall, directly beneath the centre of the elaborate chandelier which hung from the centre of the immense cupola that I'd seen from the marina. The room glowed. It glimmered with gold-trimmed walls of waxed wood in great looping, swooping art nouveau arches and ovals and orbs framing backlit stained glass and needlepoint depictions of choice highlights from the reign of Queen Victoria, including that time she slew a dragon, and the occasion on which she pulled a sword from a stone. The carpet was comprehensive and woven in gold and royal blue in a pattern which mirrored the domed ceiling. It was the sort of casino where I've always assumed I'd one day be shot by a select squad of muddy Bolsheviks.

There were eight players in the casino (counting the pianist, nine). Most were hypnotised by the roulette wheel, some were willing aces from the *vingt-et-un* dealer, and my mother was momentarily alone, wearing an ivory evening gown, a diamond necklace, matching earrings, and that predatorial look that comes upon her when she hasn't impoverished anyone at baccarat for more than ten minutes. It's becoming, somehow, on her patrician, angular features — not unlike my own, had I been constructed specifically for cutting glass. Her black hair with silver inlay was crochéd into a Chinese puzzle and, on spotting my approach, she hooked one eyebrow up two notches.

"What ho, progenitor." I kissed the proffered cheek before assuming a place across the table.

"Anty, darling, you're here already. It's only been a week since I got your letter agreeing to come — I assumed you'd still be sleeping off boat race night. That was only last month, wasn't it?" Mama appraised me with a maternal eye. "What's that you're wearing?"

"It's a white dinner jacket. Very Mediterranean, my tailor assures me."

"You look like the milkman."

"Do I now?"

"Don't be vulgar, Anty." Mama pointed at the croupier with her spare eyebrow. "How's life in London? Are the theatres, clubs, race tracks and pubs still consuming all your productive hours? You really should learn to relax, poor boy. You'll get ulcers."

"Still a tireless mainstay of the reclining classes," I assured her. "But of course, you've doubtless heard tell of my other activities."

"Quite possibly. I recall reading something about a young man who had to be rescued from the roof of Saint Botolph's in Aldgate. Was that you?"

"Of course not," I scoffed. "Wait, you did say Saint Botolph's?"

"In Aldgate."

"Of course not," I scoffed again. "Do you really mean to sit there like a marble Mama and claim to not know how I saved Lady Knebbly's parish fund-raiser in Knebbly-upon-Stomp?"

"Did you go? I'm very pleased."

"Yes, I went, and had it not been for me the society pages might have frenzied on three days of sizzling scandal rather than reporting 'a successful day, with fine weather enjoyed by all, and eighteen pounds six raised towards the new church roof.'"

"You kept your drinking to a tipsy minimum," gushed Mama. "Good boy."

"On the contrary," I said coolly. "I fell in the river. Deliberately, I hasten to add, so that I might cover for the vicar who did the same, moments earlier, after passing the morning steadying his nerves at The Cricketers."

"Didn't that just make you both look like sots?"

"Well, obviously, mother, I had the presence of mind to push Lord Knebbly in first."

"Of course."

"You raised me right," I concluded. "But in any case, I was referring more to my recent contributions to the business of the police."

"Surely they have enough to do already."

"Yes, very droll, mother," I said. "I suppose you expect me to believe that you've heard nothing of my accomplishments in Fray last year, regarding the now infamous Canterfell Codicil?"

"Have you been down to Fray? How is the major?"

"Dead."

"Well, he wasn't a young man."

"Murdered."

"He wasn't a well-liked man, either."

"You really don't know that I solved a double locked-room murder in Fray, absolved my friend Fiddles, and was instrumental in making him an earl?"

"Remind me, Anty, which of your friends is Fiddles?" asked Mama. "Is that the one who drinks too much? Or one of the others who drinks too much?"

It should be noted here that my mother's poker face has been compared, in her considerable favour, to the recently embalmed. She may well have been laughing gaily behind her steely blue eyes, or she may have been staring in blank, earnest, ignorance. She may have been suffering cardiac arrest. The woman is a marvel of stoicism.

"I take it then that you claim to know nothing of my celebrated involvement in what the papers are calling the Tale of the Tenpenny Tontine. Or how I saved Aunty Azalea from a charge of double murder at Christmas?"

"I'm afraid that I haven't spoken to your aunt since your father's funeral."

"You don't get the papers here?"

"Only the quality ones," said Mama. "But we could always place a special order if you're missing the racing odds and gossip pages."

Ask almost anyone and they'll tell you — the best time to confront your mother with your suspicions that she had your father murdered is when you first have them, the second best time is now. It was Vickers who, last year, made the connection between a known assassin and the young lady my mother had hired to be my father's secretary only days before he stumbled into the path of an electric tram at Wormwood Scrubs, but it was I who realised that if anyone was going to put my father out of my mother's misery it would be, four times out of five, my mother.

"Very well," I dismissed, "let us say for the sake of fluid conversation that you're only just now learning that I've developed something of a knack for the nobbly knock-off. I've established a rather high batting average, even if it's me saying so — there remains only one murder I have yet to solve."

Mama closed and opened her eyes. This, for my mother, was highly emotive. The granite-faced equivalent of Gielgud's 'My heart is in the coffin there with Caesar.'

"How could you possibly know about that?"

"Well, I've just told you, mother," I said. "It's my newly discovered area of expertise — the suspicious death."

Before conversation could turn any more awkward and accusatory, another player took a place at the baccarat table; a distinguished, bronze and silver chap of roughly Mama's age in a navy captain's blazer, polka-dotted ascot, vaguely military bearing and all the untamed bonhomie of a Volga boatman. He smiled the wan smile of hope for all the mercy one could expect from the four horsemen of the apocalypse and/or my mother dealing baccarat.

"Good evening, Commodore," said Mama. "May I introduce my son, Anthony. Anty, this is Pip Wairing."

"What ho, Commodore," I greeted. "That your steam-bucket in the harbour? Majestic. Thought it was the Carreras building, at first, but then I remembered that's in Camden."

"Yes, it's mine." Wairing nodded, wide-eyed, as though in that moment comprehending the awesome responsibility of boat ownership. "Do you want it? Make you a very fair price."

"Anty does not want to buy your boat, Commodore." Mother yet again pulled me from the brink of having to invent a reason to not purchase an ocean-going vessel. Doubtless she had other plans for my money. She advanced a column of ten thousand francs onto the green felt.

"Minimum stake is a thousand francs."

The croupier, a bow-tied bird with a blasé bearing, gave me a sleepy and sympathetic smile, and sold me a stack of clubby, clackity casino plaques.

There's a convivial, communal character to the betting of baccarat. The bank opens hostilities with something rich and aggressive — say ten thousand francs when a thousand would do — and if no one says 'banco', meaning they'll match the entire bet, then the other punters at the table and even the spectators chip in their bit until the offer is met. In the spirit of the game I was about to sigh 'banco' because I'm a sportsman, and just handing my mother ten thousand francs would have been, while more efficient, not entirely in the spirit of things.

The 'player' in baccarat is whoever is not clever enough to be bank nor wise enough to refuse a majority share of the bet. As a courtesy to the commodore, I said a silent farewell to six, thousand-franc plaques.

"Commodore?" Mama cast her net for the remaining four thousand.

Wairing counted his stack with the bemused resignation of the midnight gambler, inured to low rolls and anarchistic hands of cards with little in common.

"Perhaps not," he said, finally. "Experiencing something of a run of poor luck, lately."

"It's why they call them games of chance, Commodore," I said.

"That's true, isn't it?" The commodore chippered a bit at this revelation. "Just a couple bad bounces of the ball, a few unlucky deals, fourteen consecutive overdraws at *vingt-et-un*, and before you know it you've lost your entire coal budget."

"Oh, uhm, right oh," I prevaricated. "Just the way the wheel turns, sometimes."

"Quite right, Anty." The commodore studied his remaining plaques. "Doesn't go very far in explaining how we hit the reefs, coming in…" He looked up from his chips with a weary cheer "Mind you — it's not as though I could afford a new propeller, even if the wheel had gone my way."

"There you go."

"And I might not even need any coal, either, if the crew never comes back."

"Staffing troubles, Commodore?" asked Mama.

"Oh, you know, can't really blame them." The commodore raised his little stack of plaques and let them clack back down on the green felt. "Came up a little short on their wages, after having to put in at Monte Carlo when our fresh water supply somehow became home to a community of puddle frogs."

"That does sound oddly unfortunate," I agreed.

"Probably attracted by the water scorpions." The commodore shrugged. "You wouldn't believe the mooring fees in Monte Carlo."

Commodore Wairing mused on his luck, aided in the exercise with the common casino rosary of raising his chips and dropping them, one by one. Finally he seemed to enter a state of peace — I've seen this before. It's a sort of mental rubicon, a line the gambler crosses after which he's essentially daring fate to just go ahead and take it all.

The commodore tossed four plaques onto the table with all the giddy optimism of a big game fisherman casting chum onto the surface of a duck pond.

Mother dealt me two cards and two for herself. I tipped them up and gave them a peek, for form's sake. Two kings. A choice pair, you'd say, if you didn't know that according to the progressive mathematics of baccarat, two kings equals zero (or 'baccarat' — the game is named for the lowest possible score — it's as if Cricket had been called 'Out on the First Ball').

The thing about the gambler's rubicon is that he doesn't really mean it. He thinks he's fooling destiny by pretending to not care, and so destiny will lose interest and, in that moment, the gambler cleans up, cashes out, and goes home and puts it all in railway charters. Commodore Wairing glanced at me sideways, so the fates wouldn't notice, and I saw in his eyes the child-like hope he was investing in me. I called for my third card.

Another king.

I turned over my cards. Mother turned over hers. A four and a three. The croupier raked our contribution to my mother's side of the table. The commodore watched it go with a serene acquiescence, as though the universe, while imperfect, was unfolding in line with expectations.

Mama left ten thousand francs on the table.

"Monsieur…" The croupier offered me another chance to filter the face cards out of the deck.

"Banco." I didn't say that. I was going to, but something loud and excited and about shoulder height behind me said it first, and hopped into the chair next to me.

"Good evening, Deebee." My mother nodded to a coil of kinetic energy wound tightly into a ruffled shirt and swallowtail tuxedo pinned on top of a pair of shimmering leather boots. He was short and compact and he looked as though, were he to fall off his chair, he'd bounce right back. "Deebee Digby, may I present my son, Anthony."

"Call me Anty," I said and offered him my hand, which he took as though he believed the exchange to be final.

"Here at last, are you Anty?" said DeeBee with a pageantry that made me sound like 'the act you've all been waiting for…'

Deebee scattered ten plaques and my mother dealt. They each appraised their cards and then, in keeping with rules designed to limit the influence of skill, psychology, and suspense on game play, turned them over. Mama had a natural — two cards totalling nine — and Digby had six. The croupier collected another ten thousand on my mother's behalf. The commodore watched wistfully.

"Ahoy, Commodore," hailed Deebee from his side of the table. "What brings you ashore?"

"Seasick."

"You should check into the Royale," advised Deebee. "We're all scheduled up. Be here another week, at least, then it's Antibes, I think. Or is it Saint Tropez?"

"Are you one of the commodore's passengers?" I asked.

"I'm all of the commodore's passengers," corrected Deebee. "I assumed you knew who I was."

"Deebee owns the *Cirque d'Azur*," explained Mama.

"They're touring the Riviera by steam yacht."

"A circus?"

"The circus," amended Deebee. "Only floating high-wire act in the world. You didn't come down for the show?"

"Not exclusively, no," I confessed. "I'm not entirely certain what goes on at a circus. As a child I was led to believe that they were all just lesser variations of Piccadilly Circus, but I've since discovered that to be something of a departure from the facts on the ground."

"It was for your own good," claimed Mama. "You'd have only wanted to go."

"Probably," I conceded, and then confided to Deebee, "I was an inconsiderate child."

"Not the show I meant..." Deebee spoke in the low register from which the natural-born showman builds anticipation. "You can see a circus anytime..." He brought it up a notch. "Next week in Antibes. Two shows daily..." He approached the crescendo. "Or possibly Saint Tropez..." And then the big reveal. "But I'm talking about the ultimate spectacle... an execution."

"The where now?"

"Execution." Deebee returned to conversational altitude. "Of the murderer."

CHAPTER TWO

Sycophants, Unknown Aunts, and a Sudden Glance at Chance Romance

"There's been a murder?"

"I thought you knew about it," said Mama.

"Well, I didn't," I assured her.

"Then to which murder were you referring not two minutes ago?" Mama asked this with the same anodyne detachment with which she says everything murder-related.

"Papa's," I stated, I thought, the obvious.

"Your father wasn't murdered."

This was a setback. Apparently, we had been discussing two different murders when my mother had said, 'How could you possibly know about that?'

"Very well, then, who was?" I asked.

"Nobody," answered Mama.

"Malandrino the Magnificent," differed Deebee. "My headline act."

"Deebee is in show business," pointed out Mama. "I'll bet you have sawdust in your boots right now, don't you, Deebee?"

"Proudly so," replied Deebee. "What of it?"

"Show people exaggerate," said Mama to me. "You remember your Uncle Roscoe?"

"The impresario?" I recalled from my childhood. "Didn't he mount some record-setting production of Hamlet at the Victoria? With live horses and a cannon?"

"This is what Roscoe claimed, yes," said Mama without inflexion. "But it wasn't the Victoria Theatre, it was Victoria Station, and it was a puppet show."

"Let us take another tack, then," I repositioned. "Who's going to be executed?"

"A ruthless, savage killer. The likes of which the civilised world has never seen..." trumpeted Deebee. "Thumpy the elephant. He trampled Malandrino to death."

"And you mean to put Thumpy down?" I asked, aghast.

"Of course I'm not going to 'put Thumpy down'," scorned Deebee. "I've lost my centre ringer. The show's biggest single draw. Got to recover some of my investment. I'm going to execute Thumpy, in the most spectacular fashion possible, and sell tickets to the event."

I turned this over for a moment, internally, and outwardly I probably appeared to stare at Deebee in blinking, blank astonishment. "This is easily the most appalling thing I've heard since learning that the hotel manager's name is Beaujolais."

"I struggled with that myself," sympathised Mama. "I just call him Rémy."

"Me too," I said. "Does he call you Mama?"

"Madame."

"Oh, right, of course. Setting that aside, Deebee, has there been any sort of investigation? Has this elephant received due process under French law?"

"There's no doubt about what happened, Anty," replied Mama on his behalf. "Malandrino, or whatever it is he called himself, let himself into the cage and for whatever reason — doubtless some perfectly defensible line of thinking from Thumpy's perspective — the elephant stepped on him. Repeatedly, by all evidence."

"Well, exactly," I redirected to Deebee. "Thumpy might have been acting in self-defence."

"It's an elephant. Have you ever seen an elephant?"

"I have not," I said with admirable reserve. "As mentioned, I endured an uncommonly deprived childhood. Nevertheless, one of God's creatures, and all that, in exactly the same way that terriers, goats, cows and crows are, and that mosquitos and hornets are not. In any case, as you appear to be pointing out, aren't elephants enormous? How are you planning to execute one?"

"Firing squad." Deebee squinted as he considered this, in the manner of the more hard-nosed villain, contemplating the particulars of a pending orphanage foreclosure. "It's more dignified. Also, there's a count-down — great for building suspense. Hanging's probably not viable — not sure I could build a gallows that big — economically, I mean." He brightened as a new horror came to him. "There's always drowning."

"I can tell you're a visionary, Deebee," I said. "Surely, then, you can see your way clear to giving this elephant the chance to argue his case before a jury of his peers."

"Of course." Deebee grasped the banks of the baccarat table in a seizure of inspiration. "Let the punters decide — will it be guillotine, hanging, or, or..." He anchored himself against waves of genius. "...a surprise third way. And we'll hold a raffle to choose an audience member to pull the switch."

"Yes, that sounds delightfully barbaric," I said. "But what I meant was that Thumpy is entitled to a full examination of the facts. When did it happen?"

"Nobody knows, for sure," said Deebee. "Saturday night, during the launch party."

"This is when the victim was last seen, I take it. What time was that?"

"No one can really say." The commodore spoke up and then handed off to Deebee and Mama.

"I don't recall seeing him on the boat at all," said Mama.

"He was on board, all right," said Deebee. "I certainly saw

him around ten, when the fireworks started. He was with the biddies — one of them probably saw him leave."

"The biddies?" I queried.

"Bidelia Mimpley and Myrtle Biddicomb. Known collectively as the biddies. " My mother nodded towards a pair perched like owls on stools at the bar, best described as notable for how much they looked like two women who would be collectively known as the biddies.

"Camp followers," added Deebee. "Never miss a show, either of them."

"So he was still alive at ten, at the very least," I concluded.

"Closer to eleven, actually," submitted the commodore. "It takes a good twenty minutes to get ashore, then another twenty to get to the other side of the island. Thumpy's cage is on the beach."

"I see. So Malandrino departed the yacht — how is your boat christened, by the way, Commodore?"

"Little Miss Fortune."

"Of course. So Malandrino departed Little Miss Fortune no earlier than ten and... how does one get ashore?"

"Skiffs," answered the commodore. "The marina's too shallow to moor, so we're anchored some distance out."

"So he goes ashore, in the middle of the launch party, and goes to visit an elephant?" I observed. "Does that not strike anyone else as odd?"

"In a manner of speaking, it was his elephant," said Deebee.

"What manner is that?"

"It was part of his new act. This is why Malandrino was magnificent. He was no mere clown," enthused Deebee. "Never the same act two seasons in a row. Last year alone, in the same year, Mandrino is the first ever to juggle live chinchillas *and* he breaks the record for most synchronised dancing bears in a high-wire act."

"There was a previous record?"

"Five," replied Deebee. "A record established in 1926 by none other than Malandrino the Magnificent."

"Do bears like synchronised dancing on a high wire?" I asked.

"Love it," Deebee assured me. "Never met a bear who didn't want to get a foothold in the entertainment business. Elephants, maybe a little less so. Thumpy was having a hard time with his role. Probably why Malandrino went to work with him, what with opening night in only four days."

"What was Thumpy's role, exactly?"

"Not sure. I've never seen an entire rehearsal, but Malandrino was very big on your high concepts. Take the bear act. The whole thing plays out as a fable of Mandrino's own invention — he's Rasputin, see, and the bears are the entire Romanov family, that he turned into bears so they could escape the revolution."

"And you don't know what the concept was that Malandrino was working with Thumpy," I said.

"It'll be something along similar lines," speculated Deebee. "The elephant was supposed to be scared of Malandrino, so he'd jump through hoops or tap dance or whatever he was told, and of course the whole time Malandrino is dressed as a mouse."

"Very well, but why a mouse, and why of course a mouse?"

"Well, it's funny, right?" Deebee cast about the table for agreement and, by and large, seemed to get it. "Because elephants are afraid of mice."

"They are?"

"I don't know." Deebee said this as one oppressed by the complexity of the questions. "They're supposed to be, that's all that matters. Anyway, that's how I figure Malandrino was rehearsing with Thumpy — when we found him the next day, he was wearing his mouse costume."

"Just a tic." I held up a hand the rough size and shape of a tic. "Am I to understand that, in summation, the night before last, Thumpy the elephant trampled to death a man dressed as a mouse?"

"In just so many words," confirmed Deebee.

As he spoke, a neon dandy in a burgundy tuxedo took the seat next to the commodore and mispronounced, *"Bonsoir, chers amis."* He smiled widely and toothily, like one who practises wide, toothy smiles for hours in the mirror, and appraised the table through a monocle while he fitted a cigarette into an ebony holder the length of his arm. His cement-coloured hair shone generously of chicken fat, and his moustache curled in waxen whirls.

"Tot of rot, Commodore?" Deebee stood as the new arrival sat. "It's on me." Without another word, they retired to the bar.

"I thought they'd never leave," said the toothy smile. "Evening, Mrs Boisjoly..." The monocle focused on me. "...stranger."

"This is my son, Anthony," said Mama. "Anthony, this is Max Minefield."

"Minefield?" I marvelled. "Not really."

"A *nom de guerre."* Max lit his cigarette at arm's length. "I'm a critic. Doubtless you've read my work."

"I don't think I have, in fact, and I read all the reviews."

"Pleased to be of service," assumed Max. "If a cutting critique can stop one man seeing a poor performance, our noble work is done."

"I never read anything until I've seen the show," I clarified. "I tend to like just about everything. Do you do musicals? Comedies? Musical-comedies?"

"Circus. I specialise in the big top." Max smoothed his moustache with the slow precision of a skilled sculptor making a Father Christmas candle.

"You're a circus critic?"

"I'm *the* circus critic, Anthony." Max drew on his slim cigarette holder with such intensity that his monocle popped out. He exhaled thin streams of smoke through his nose. "I single-handedly foreshortened the Blackpool to Brighton tour of the Toppler Brothers Big Top Show last year with the line, 'Were it not for the over-priced entry and talentless tumblers, I'd have believed myself to be watching a production of one of Dostoyevsky's darker dramas, which might have proved more amusing.' Clever, don't you think? I have a copy of it, if you'd like to read the rest."

"Tolstoy."

"I beg your pardon?"

"You mean Tolstoy, I think," I said. "Dostoyevsky didn't write plays."

"No matter…" Max waved away the oversight with his cigarette wand. "…the tour was foreshortened. But you say you're interested in the theatre…"

"Oh, rather," I said. "Have you seen *Hold Everything* at the Palace?"

"I have not. I'm a critic. I have no time to sit through entire productions. But as you're interested in theatre, Anthony, I have a rather intriguing proposition for you…"

"Max…" intervened Mama, with the tone she would employ with Papa when she caught him setting the clocks to the cocktail hour. "Anty does not want to hear your proposition."

"But he's just said he's interested in the theatre," protested Max.

"Anty has many interests," agreed Mama. "Theatre, of course, but also horse racing and boat racing, not to mention drinking at the horse races, boat races, and at intermission. From the moment it starts at four in the afternoon, his day is an unbroken series of enterprising endeavours." Mama set a sternly meaningful stack of plaques on the table. "Banco, Max?"

Of course, by then I wanted nothing more than to know Max's proposal but, like the reckoning with Mama regarding my father's passing, it would have to join the queue.

"Did you know Malandrino the Magnificent, Max?" I asked, as my mother dealt the cards.

"Of course." Max tipped up his hand and produced a sly, enigmatic smile that said 'I have baccarat' as clearly as if he'd spoken the words aloud. "I know everyone in the business — card please." Mama dealt him a queen. "Of course, I know what you're thinking — it's what everyone's thinking."

"What is everyone thinking, Max?" I asked.

"That I killed him."

"Point of fact, most people are claiming that he was trampled by an elephant." I paused to watch Mama turn over a natural eight and Max to reveal, as expected, zero. "Your name has yet to come up. Why are people saying that you killed him?"

"Because I did," explained Max. "I mean, indirectly. Malandrino was driven to perfect his elephant act to win my approval, you see, after I pilloried his dancing bears last year with the line, 'Were it not for the discordant dancing bears and bizarrely bearded Malandrino, I might have believed myself at a staging of the *Storming of the Summer Palace,* which would at least have been rehearsed.' It goes on, but that's the bull's-eye. I have a copy…"

"Winter Palace."

"Nevertheless." Once again Max Minefield waved his wand of indifference. "It's my penetrating prose that drove Malandrino to careless extremes. He was rehearsing the act when it happened, you know."

"So I understand — did you see him that night?"

"Briefly. We exchanged a few pleasantries on the boat." Max watched the croupier reward my mother's luck with his chips. "I told him how much I looked forward to seeing his new act, and he told me how much he looked forward to dancing on my grave. Then he offered to throw me overboard."

"Are you calling *suivi,* Max?" Mama was asking, in the language of baccarat, if Max wished to claim his right to lose another ten thousand francs.

"I think not." Max unwound from the table — he stubbed out his cigarette and filed away his holder and monocle. "There's a team of Brazilian acrobats premiering in Marseille next week, and I really must get started on my first impressions."

"What a delightful circle of friends you've established here, Mumster. I look forward to meeting the biddies — kidnappers, are they?" We watched Max ooze out the shimmering casino doorway. As he did, he executed an obsequious little bow to two dramatically, differently and indifferently dazzling women. They schooned into the room like flapper flagships, all feathers and fringes and folding fans and a musical way of moving, as though accompanied by a brass section and an all-male chorus dressed as, say, sailors. The pair swung back their blonde billows in unison — or possibly not, I may well be idealising the moment a bit — and cat-walked towards the baccarat table. To my delight, they assumed places to my left and right and elevated me with their regard.

"This must be little Anthony. How he's grown." The vintage model, roughly my mother's age, audited my progress from my left.

"And what a spiffing specimen of the species he's grown into," adjudged the later release, nearer my age, on my right. "He looks like a collar advertisement, reacting to a car backfiring."

A fair assessment from a fair maiden. The ladies were golden-haired and blue-eyed and they both had a winking sort of intelligence about them. The daughter was slighter and more lythe, like a panther with years of ballet training, and she met my gaze with an elated, open-mouthed smile, as though meeting me and me alone was an unanticipated delight. The small but energetic community of butterflies that live in my stomach awoke with a start and instantly organised themselves into a riot.

"Anthony, this is your Aunt Jacqueline and her daughter, Chadwick," said my mother off-handedly.

"I have an Aunt Jacqueline?" I asked.

"I married your Uncle Ambrose, after his poor wife died, when was that Cleo?" Aunt Jacqueline said to my mother whose first name, incidentally, is Cleopatra.

"I have an Uncle Ambrose?" I asked.

"Not anymore." Aunt Jacqueline lit a cigarillo with a high flame and a flourish. "He died in '24, the poor dear. Ballooning accident."

"That is unfortunate," I sympathised. "I've had accidents with balloons. I had no idea they could be fatal."

"Hot air balloon, Anty," clarified Mama.

"Oh, right," I said. "That makes much more sense. So, what brings you to Cap Royale?"

"Boredom," exhaled Jacqueline in a plume of blue smoke.

"Excitement," differed Chadwick simultaneously, and traded the croupier a hundred pounds for a stack of plaques. "The circus is in town."

"We simply had to get away from Cap Ferrat and that frightful lech." Jacqueline fluttered a feather at the barman, who had been staring at her anyway. "What was his name, Chaddy? That Belgian fellow."

"King Albert."

"That's it. Kept offering to build me a villa. Who needs another villa?"

"So, when we learned that Aunty Cleo was just up the coast, we slipped away under cover of cocktails." Chadwick held up a 'stand by for instructions' hand to the barman as he skidded up next to her. Then she pointed at each of us in turn, starting with Mama, and said, "Whisky and plain water, vodka martini with crushed ice and lime zest, whisky and a whisper, and I'll have the same."

"How the devil…?" I swooned.

"It's a gift," said Chadwick. "It's a good thing we came when we did, or we'd have missed the launch party — cocktails, fireworks, an acrobat, death by elephant, they even had a seafood barbeque, right on board the yacht."

"You were there for that then, were you?" I asked.

"We certainly were," said Chadwick. "Tuna, swordfish, squid… the works."

"Did you happen to see Malandrino the Magnificent on board?"

"Uhm, maybe…Mom?" Chadwick passed the question to her mother.

"One clown looks very much like the rest, to me," said Jacqueline. "Circus performers and otherwise."

"But you couldn't say what time he left the boat," I deduced.

"I'd say, give or take…" Chadwick pursed her lips in reflection. "…sometime before he died."

I had no recollection of any Uncle Ambrose, which meant

that he was some distant cousin of my mother's. In any case, Jacqueline married him later in life, and Chadwick was not his daughter nor any sort of blood relation. And so, in light of her gifts and fashion and poise and cocktail prejudices and general angle of approach, I was left with no choice. However, before I could ask her to marry me a crowd of Deebees and commodores had formed.

"Jacqueline, put those drinks on my tab." Deebee bounced into the seat next to my future mother-in-law.

"Well, obviously, Deebee," said Jacqueline with wonder in her voice. "How else does one pay for one's drinks?"

"Got a big idea, Jaqs, and it needs your special touch," enthused Deebee. "I need a draw for a main event — can you get your chum, Prince Louis, to be my guest of honour?"

"Probably. He owes me a favour." Jacqueline drew meditatively on her cigarillo. "The only problem, as I see it Deebee, is that *I* don't owe *you* one."

"I'll make it worth your while," promised the mogul.

"What's the occasion?"

"Tell him it's a world's first — an execution, and we want him to pull the switch."

"What switch?"

"The power switch," revelled Deebee. "In four days, we execute Thumpy the elephant — by electrocution."

CHAPTER THREE

The Relevance of the Evidence of the Reticence of Elephants

Waking up between crisp linen sheets on a deep four-poster in a luxury suite on a summer's day on the Riviera is a fully rigged, morning-going adventure. The air is a poetic, pelagic perfume of bougainvillaea blossoms, pine trees and salty seas. The soft, southern sun seeps in from all directions in a uniquely luxurious shade of turquoise that seems, somehow, expensive. The ambient temperature adjusts itself to taste. Gulls and herons whinge and squabble and somewhere — somewhere quite near, as it turns out — something explodes.

The windows rattled and the boom echoed like thunder, but what I could see of the sky from my bed was cloudless cyan. As it happens, the curious occurrence coincided with Vickers' morning mercy mission — the tea tray.

"Did you hear that, Vickers?" I asked.

"Yes, sir. It was the cannon."

"Cannon, eh?" I shifted into tea tray docking position. "Are we under attack by pirates? If so, I think we should at least consider joining up with them. Seize the saga of the seven seas, far from the dictates of civil society and my mother."

Vickers opened the immense double doors leading to my bedroom balcony (as opposed to my larger, salon balcony) and issued one of those secret, servant-to-servant bows to someone down below.

"Monsieur Beaujolais, the hotel manager, has just fired the midday cannon."

"I assume that means it's midday," I concluded. "Doubtless Rémy feared I would oversleep. Have a chat with him, will you Vickers, and set him straight on the strict Boisjoly regimen."

"The cannon is fired every day at noon, sir," explained Vickers. "The tradition has been practised for several decades, and was instituted as a commemorative of the peninsula's role in defending neighbouring Nice against naval attack from Savoyard, Genovese, and Sardinian forces, respectively."

"This little island was a maritime stronghold?"

"More of a pawn, historically." Vickers occupied himself with the day's wardrobe as he spoke. "The cape was conquered on some four hundred occasions. The cannon was fired to indicate total capitulation to the enemy and, for a time, was very nearly a daily occurrence."

Vickers had been my father's valet before me and his father's before him and so on, dating back to the invention of Boisjolys or valets, whichever came first. His actual age is probably lost to the mists of time and his memory for all things recent — if my adult lifetime can be considered recent — is a delightful scatterbox of snatches and surprises. However everything that took his notice — meaning, everything — up until a very finely defined line in time, is readily and thoroughly on tap. As a random example, while recounting in granular detail that which he knew of Cap Royale from the days, years ago, he spent here with my parents, he was packing my trunk.

"I think we might linger on a few days yet, Vickers," I said. "There's been a development."

"Indeed, sir?"

"In very deed," I confirmed. "An unexplained death in most unusual circumstances. I say unexplained — everyone seems to have an explanation ready to hand, but I don't like it. Not least because the presumed guilty party is incapable of instructing defence counsel."

Vickers stood in the glow of sunlight swelling through the balcony door, that adrift distance in his eyes known throughout

Kensington as the Vickers gaze.

"Are we discussing... Mrs Boisjoly?"

"No, Vickers, we're talking about another, more recent unplanned departure," I said. "The scheduled reckoning with my mother regarding my father's rapid deceleration will have to wait."

"How is madam?" Vickers returned to mismatching my suit.

"Unchanged, I'm sorry to report," I said. "Do you know she's managed to remain entirely unaware of my activities for over a year? She's my mother — that would almost have to be deliberate, wouldn't it?"

"I couldn't possibly say, sir."

"No, of course not, Vickers, I'll just assume on your behalf that you agree with me," I informed him. "Incidentally, do I have an Aunt Jacqueline?"

"Not to my knowledge, sir."

"What about an Uncle Ambrose?"

"Ambrose Quillfeather was your mother's second cousin," casually recited Vickers. "He died in a ballooning accident in America in 1909. He was endeavouring to land on the roof of the Times building."

"Tricky manoeuvre, I expect."

"Manifestly so," intoned Vickers. "Mister Quillfeather did manage to land on the roof but, alas, the balloon did not."

"Well, apparently he left a widow and an absolute corker of a step-daughter. Witty, wise, well-assembled and, uhm, whisky-drinking." I sipped nostalgically on my tea. "Connected, too, by all accounts. Her mother knows Louis."

"His Serene Highness Prince Louis II of Monaco?"

"That's the chappy. Took my shirt and collar off me at baccarat in '24. She's going to get him to help murder an elephant."

"I find that difficult to credit, sir."

"No, now I say it out loud, I don't think much of her chances either," I said. "Nevertheless, the execution is going to go ahead in three days unless I can determine what really happened on Saturday night. What can you tell me about the beach on the west side of the island?"

"It is rarely used as such, owing to inconvenient access," recalled Vickers. "The beach is in a deep cove, most easily achieved by boat, except at night."

"Why not at night?"

"The currents. On a dark night the land and sea and, most notably, reefs can become indistinguishable."

"Oh, right, I remember Pilque saying something about that."

"Most guests prefer to bathe on the point," continued Vickers. "The high rocks serve as diving platforms, and the natural caves as changing cabins. Shall I lay out your bathing costume?"

"No, actually. Something light, yet inquisitive." I set aside the tray and slipped out of bed. "I wish to be taken seriously. On the other hand, I wish to wear my straw boater. What are your thoughts, Vickers?"

"The sun is very strong today, and the Boisjolys enjoy a most noble complexion."

I walked beneath my straw boater across the tiled square before the hotel. It's a magnificent square. The tiles are in a checkerboard pattern and the east and west sides are bordered with immense palm trees, and at the centre is a fountain, featuring a porcelain Queen Victoria riding a team of dolphins. I paused there for a moment to reflect on the good fortune of all concerned that Her Majesty never saw it.

"Good afternoon, Mister Boisjoly." The biddies orbited into view as I circled the fountain.

"What ho, what ho," I replied. "Miss Mimpley and Miss Biddicomb, I understand, or Miss Biddicomb and Miss Mimpley. Mother pointed you out last night, but stopped short of scars, tattoos, and identifying characteristics."

"I'm Biddicomb," said what I would describe as the flamboyant biddy. She had a daring, come-what-may look to her marcelled hair, little round glasses, and sunshine yellow sack dress paired with a straw knitting bag embroidered with a meadow scene — the spinster version of the chap who recites original poetry in the basement of the union hall.

"We saw you at the casino last night, Mister Boisjoly." This would be, having eliminated Biddicomb, Miss Mimpley in flowery number and matching parasol. Mimpley struck me as the serious biddy, with a confidential, contemplative nature — sort of woman you want on hand to ensure the church bake sale goes off without police involvement.

"Gambling is a vice, Mister Boisjoly," pointed out Mimpley.

"Not the way I do it," I said. "More in the line of a charitable contribution to the upkeep of British racecourses and European casinos. You don't play?"

"We're dedicated spectators," explained Biddicomb.

"So I understand. Mister Digby tells me that you never miss a performance of the circus."

The biddies looked at one another and then at their shoes.

"Not the circus, Mister Boisjoly," said Mimpley.

"It was Malandrino the Magnificent that we loved," completed Biddicomb.

"Yes, I understand that his acts were record-making and breaking," I said. "I myself have never seen a circus performance, owing to a disadvantaged childhood that I'd prefer not discuss…"

"Oh, no, Mister Boisjoly…" said Mimpley.

"We very much enjoyed his acts," continued Biddicomb. "But when we say we loved Malandrino, we mean that we loved him…"

"Wholly…" decorated Mimpley.

"And completely," summed up Biddicomb.

"Oh, right, well…" I think I'd have been better prepared for the biddies to claim that they were the Wright Brothers. "My condolences."

"Oh, he was a cad, Mister Boisjoly." Biddicomb said this as though to Mimpley, who nodded in agreement.

"Callous."

"You'd say he had a cold, cold heart…"

"…if he had a heart."

"I understand that you were on the boat the night of the tragedy," I shifted, dexterously, sideways.

"Such a lovely party." Biddicomb rebounded instantly.

"There were fireworks…"

"…and a seafood barbeque."

"We'd never tasted swordfish before."

"Did you happen to note what time Malandrino left the yacht?" I asked.

"It's difficult to say…"

"We didn't speak to him."

"Oh? Why not?"

"She won't let me." Biddicomb cocked her slightly towards Mimpley.

"And neither will she." Mimpley subtly indicated Biddicomb.

"I see," I claimed, though something in their account struck me, not so much as untrue, but unexpected, like a second king of spades, or a midday cannon. "Can you tell me this, though, was it a dark night?"

"Oh, yes." The biddies spoke and nodded simultaneously. "Very dark, indeed."

On a very dark night, indeed, Malandrino would have crossed the island on foot to get to the beach, dash him. I would obviously have to do the same, if I was going to give any of the elephants in my care anything like due diligence.

The square ends in a panorama plateau, with a broad view of the horizon, a small ceremonial cannon, and steps leading to paths weaving down and around and through the rocky wall of the point. These partially natural and partially man-made shelves criss-cross eventually to the water and along the way provide access to caves and diving platforms. Millions of years of erosion have carved a little harbour into the point, deep and diveable and comparatively calm bordered, as it was, by breakwaters in the form of towering mushrooms of rock.

Between the gates of the breakwaters, a lone swimmer slid smoothly through the water towards shore and, on a final, forceful stroke, glided up to the rocks. Chadwick Quillfeather, in a clingy, belted, knee-length bathing costume, sprung from the water and swung her hair like a victory flag. I lost my balance and sense of three-dimensional space, briefly, and all things real and imagined took on a pinkish hue.

I was brought back to drab reality by a curious observation — she was with a man. Or at any rate, there was a chap lingering about on the rock. He was in a black, silk suit — wholly inappropriate for a day in the sun and the poor fish didn't even have a straw boater. I couldn't see his face, but I imagined it to be a greasy, obsequious, intruding sort of dial he presented to Chadwick as he offered her a towel which, I'm sorry to report, she accepted. She then appeared to pinch his cheek, causing him to turn coyly away and reveal himself to be the sleepy-eyed croupier from last night's baccarat table.

There are probably rules against this sort of fraternising, but it's never been in my nature to do the headmaster's dirty work. I made mental note to challenge the croupier to a duel, when next at my leisure.

The path curved around the island to the east, where it sloped gently towards the marina, and to the west, where it disappeared into thick foliage.

The jungle was as dense and impenetrable as the back four shelves of a second-hand bookshop. The path was navigable enough, though, and had recently been coiffed and manicured. As I safaried deeper, I was enveloped by a happy, heavy, humid atmosphere and that otherworldly green glow of a tropical sun filtered through a canopy of palm, pine and parasols of cypress. The woods whistled with swallow and cicada and, distantly, the hush and rush of the tide.

Presently, the path wound back and forth on itself as it inclined towards the sea and I found myself at the water's edge on a stony beach at the bottom of a wall of rock, clawed out of the side of the island by volcano or glacier or some improbable conspiracy of the two. Hence the beach was enclosed and large enough to serve as the stage of a floating circus. Presumably in anticipation thereof, there were scattered wagons and barrels and crates, tents and trailers, and an open-topped cage the size of the orchestra pit of the Criterion Theatre. Within, looking at me with a moving combination of hope and despair, was a saggy, baggy, grey elephant. I knew that elephants were huge, but until actually seeing one there's just no comprehending the immensity of something as big as a bus but alive, with ears like bedsheets, legs like palm trees, an absurd, animated hose of a nose, and sad, sad eyes. He raised his trunk in a listless wave and then let it drop to the floor of his cage.

The last mark left on this world by Malandrino the Magnificent was a horrid great stain on a sheet of canvas which spread over the straw floor beneath Thumpy. There was also a trough of hay and watermelons, an immense ball, and plinths of varying sizes.

Thumpy watched me as I circumnavigated the cage. I fancied he was more curious than anything else, until I encountered an equipment stand housing a long trumpet, a set of stilts, and a number of whips of differing dimensions and abominations. I don't know what caused me to reach out — probably the same feral instinct that compels a man to linger and listen when Snooters Snowsill-Willit reckons he's had enough gin to recite *Casabianca* — but for whatever reason I plucked up for examination one of the whips. This was a nasty variation on the theme of the cat-o-nine-tails, with fewer tails and more brass spikes.

Thumpy uttered a surprisingly discreet gasp for an animal his size and with an even more surprising swiftness, he leapt onto the big ball and, more astoundingly still, balanced himself there. He juttered and shuddered and focused on the job at hand, but simultaneously maintained a wide-eyed appeal for approval.

"Oh, I say, Thumpy old man." Without thinking things through I held up the whip. "You can't think I'd use this."

He did. Most feathered, furred, and phenomenally large animals assume, correctly, that they could easily touch me for ten pounds. Some trauma in Thumpy's past, however, had trained out of him the fundamental instinct which causes all good-natured creatures to assume the best of Boisjoly. His focus on the whip, Thumpy stepped off the ball with his front thumper and, amazingly, raised his other three feet in the air. And still he regarded me with one imploring eye.

I placed the diabolical device back on the rack and held up both hands in the most commonly accepted form of the inter-species sign for 'I'm not a cold-blooded sadist.'

I wandered back around to the sea-view side of the cage while Thumpy returned to earth and a more natural state of serene melancholy.

"Speaking as your only friend on the island, Thumps old thing," I said. "I have to be honest — the evidence weighs heavily against you."

Thumpy and I both regarded the horrific stain on the canvas and in the next moment the poor chap trumpeted a deafening great bleat and leapt up on a plinth and raised himself further onto his toes. Completing this picture of a colossus in terror, he rolled his trunk up after him. He rapidly swapped his attention between me and something on the canvas and I had to squint to see it — a tiny mouse had scurried out of the straw and was beneath the plinth, making faces at Thumpy.

The gate was secured with a heavy chain and immense lock, but the mouse was thankfully close to my side of the cage. I reached through the bars, took hold of a bit of canvas, lifted, and then shook the sheet like a rug. Even disregarding the instant effect on Thumpy the results were enormously satisfying. The mouse was launched into a high, long arc — which Thumpy followed with increasing relief — and then it disappeared into a bail of hay outside the cage.

Thumpy stepped down from the plinth and waddled slowly towards me. His enormous eyes had the hint of hopeful cheer of the oppressed recognising an ally. He put his trunk between the bars and gave me a playful shove that nearly dislocated my shoulder.

"You've taught me two extraordinary things, today, Thumpy," I said, amazed. "Elephants really are afraid of mice — at any rate one of you is — and, directly or otherwise, Malandrino the Magnificent was murdered by human hand."

CHAPTER FOUR

A Yacht Fraught with Lots of Plots

It's about this point in the performance that I'd normally be wiring London or tripping over the inevitable inspector therefrom. Here I was in France, though, with no notion how to send a cable off the island, never mind direct it to *Le champ d'ecosse,* or whatever it is the French call Scotland Yard. In any case, the foundation of my entire case rested on a mouse upon whose cooperation I felt I could not rely.

I proceeded, therefore, to the broad, bright, brass-lined tea room of the Riviera Royale, and the key to my first line of enquiry.

"What ho, Commodore," I publicly addressed across the sun-dappled, glass-walled but otherwise Victorian-cluttered parlour. Commodore Wairing sat forward in a high-backed chair, hovering over a silver tea set.

"Hullo, Anty," the commodore looked up to say and then returned to clattering about the teapot with a spoon.

"Any luck?" I asked, taking another high-backed seat across from him. "What are you using for bait?"

"Trying to get the tea ball out. The little chain broke." In that moment the spoon fell into the pot. The commodore gazed forlornly after it.

"I'll cue the understudy, shall I?" I offered. Rémy had followed me into the tea room and was now standing by.

"Same again, Rémy," I said. "Extra cup, stouter chain."

33

"At full frisky, Anty." Rémy swept away the tray and was gone.

"The staff call you by your first name?" wondered Wairing.

"We go way back, Rémy and me," I said. "Though I feel like it was only yesterday, around nine. Talking of arrivals on Cap Royale, Commodore, have you any idea how Deebee managed to get an elephant onto the beach?"

"Barge." Wairing had the answer at the ready, and seemed as impressed as I should have been. "The poor beast travels by train and then they use a great river barge to get him to the beach. Or that was the plan, at any rate."

"The plan for what?"

"The tour. It's a floating circus. We pitch up to these heaving tourist towns, run the high-wire from the boat to the shore so the sea is the safety net, and all the acrobats and fire-eaters and elephants and whatnot are on the beach. Very quick to set up and tear down. Very economical, compared to your traditional travelling circus, and it's got a ready audience."

"Deebee sells tickets to the beach?"

Wairing nodded. "Rather ingenious, isn't it? Two shows daily. Then there are the concessions."

"Ah, yes, of course." I nodded knowingly. "The concessions."

"The hotels and casinos — as often as not, their guests can watch the circus for nothing. Deebee negotiates a percentage of the day's receipts." Something in this caused the commodore to gaze sadly out the panoramic window of the tea room. "That's my share. It's how I'm meant to be paid for use of the yacht."

"Meant to?"

"Just a bit of poor luck, last season... staff strike at the Majestic... some sort of casino swindle at l'Ambassadeur... ptomaine outbreak at the Regal..." Wairing paused here for the installation of a new tea tray.

Rémy poured two even cups, wished us, "Good tasty," and wheeled away.

"...the Impérial closed for renovations... so did the Spléndide..."

"Doubtless this season will be more fortuitous," I suggested.

"It would almost have to be, wouldn't it?" said the commodore. "At least I won't have an elephant to mind. They eat a surprising amount... I suppose not, really, for an elephant, but I was surprised, at any rate."

"Was Thumpy somehow your responsibility?"

"No, not really." The commodore carefully stirred his tea. "Just cleaning and feeding."

"Is there much else to taking care of an elephant?"

"I suppose not, now I take inventory." Wairing grimaced into space at this galling realisation. "I somehow managed to agree that Thumpy was technically a passenger. Probably one of the reasons the crew quit."

"Then who was minding Thumpy?"

"The mug in front of you." The commodore indicated himself with a teaspoon. "That's why, of course, it was me that found poor Malandrino the morning after."

"In the elephant's cage," I surmised.

"Frightful mess. Have you ever seen someone that's been trampled by an elephant?"

"I have not, but I have seen an elephant, and I can guess the impression one could make if he put his back into it. What was Thumpy doing?"

"Rather cowering, if I had to put a word to it." The commodore looked to the skies for reminders. "He seemed to know what he'd done, and that he probably shouldn't have."

"Was the cage locked?"

"It was. I recall, because the moment I turned the key, the padlock fell on my foot."

"Of course."

"It's a big lock, too."

"I expect it needed to be," I said. "And Malandrino had a key on his person?"

"Must have done. You don't think I searched the remains, do you? Not much *to* search, if I'd had the stomach for it — good show the mouse costume was a one-piece."

"Why didn't you just wrap the whole thing up in the canvas sheet?" I asked.

"That's exactly what we did do, once the coroner chap had his look-in."

"Did you? There's a canvas sheet on the floor of the cage now, and it rather looks like it was host to a strikingly similar event."

"It was." The commodore nodded grimly and steeled his nerves with a sip of sweet tea. "There were two canvas sheets over a layer of straw. I thought it made a nice mattress sort of affair for Thumpy."

"Most considerate," I said. "You didn't see anything else unusual? Another boat, for instance?"

"Another boat? How many did you expect?"

"Well, yours, at least, and I wondered if Malandrino might have gone there by boat as well."

The commodore shook his head slowly and certainly, his eyes closed for fullness of effect. "Too dangerous for a boat in these currents at night, and I prefer to walk regardless of the hour." He opened his eyes and regarded me sincerely and gravely. "Can't stand boats."

"I wondered at my fortune running into you here," I said. "Are you staying on shore?"

"Deebee's idea." The commodore cheered marginally. "He's paying for it, and he's stumping for a delivery of coal."

"That's a bit of good fortune."

"Is it?" The commodore gazed out the broad, bevelled glass front of the tea room. I followed his eye to the harbour and the majestic profile of Little Miss Fortune. "Sure you wouldn't like to buy a boat? It's in excellent nick, apart from the propeller. And the generator. And the bilge pump — not sure what's wrong there. Can a bilge pump go backwards?"

"You know, until this moment I hadn't really considered purchasing a yacht." This was, in the main, the truth — I had never seriously considered buying a yacht, and never would. "Perhaps a tour of the tub might help move the matter along."

The tea room trickles out onto the same cobbled courtyard as the casino. This in turn spills down the hill in a wobbly, tree-lined road towards the marina, which is Cap Royale's commercial hub and hive — there was a bait shop, a dry dock, a small café, and a smaller grocer. Stretching into the water were two standing docks at which were moored fishing and flitting fleets, and to our right a path led back up the hill towards the rocky bathing cove. This was all wrapped around a petite, pastoral, provençal square ornamented with palm trees, bistro tables and chairs and parasols, afternoon drinkers and the nets, pikes, poles and pails of their unrushed trade. The sun was still above the casino cupola, so the harbour dazzled and danced in white and blue, and the air smelled of warm winds and wanderlust.

We selected a little outboard skiff and, including getting the motor started and fumbling about and finally remembering to cast off, then crossing the deceptively wide expanse to Little Miss Fortune, it was indeed a full twenty minutes before we arrived at a floating jetty moored to the port side of the yacht. It's not really my strongest suit, navigation, but standing on the jetty and gazing back at the port I judged the distance to be approximately far — perhaps the distance from the Ritz to Buckingham Palace, but covered entirely in seawater.

We tied up in company of another half-dozen passenger dories and climbed an ingenious hinged stairway that rose and ebbed with the jetty. What awaited me at the top of the gangway was beyond my maddest childhood misconceptions.

All manner of circus magic was arranged according to some enchanted programme of progressively bigger, brighter, bolder, and brasher stunts. From bow to stern, there were cables, nets, and trampolines. There were perplexing piles of props and pipes and pins for the jugglers, flashes, flares, flammables and fuels for the fire eaters, and a lengthening array of glistening sabres and scimitars to meet the demands of the most discerning sword swallower. There was an immense rubber ball on which an elephant could balance and a cannon with fire and brimstone livery that was big enough to launch an immense rubber ball on which an elephant could balance. There were stilts and unicycles and stilted unicycles. There was stacked racked seating and barrels and buckets and clown shoes and head-dresses and top hats.

"Commodore," I announced. "I would like to buy your boat."

"Really?"

Even as I spoke, my eye was drawn to the big rubber ball on which an elephant could balance, and I knew that I had lost sight of the objective. Thumpy's doleful, hopeful countenance came to me, saying 'what price the innocent?' Then Vickers' lost and bewildered expression hove into my mind's eye, saying 'I have misplaced all your collar studs, sir, but have found this lorgnette.' He wouldn't adapt well to circus life, Vickers. Nor yacht life, for that matter.

"No, not really," I geared down. "Or, rather, not just yet. Let's have a look at the staterooms, shall we?"

"You can see mine."

"Ah ha," I declared. "Precisely what we must not do. Chap I know from my club, Kegs Kellogg, once bought a house in Mayfair entirely on the strength of a visit to the master bedroom. Turned out, the place backed onto a brewery."

"Oh, right, I understand."

"Yes, pure good fortune, but it could have been anything," I said. "Place might have shared a back garden with a tannery. Or a member of the House of Lords. Then where would poor Kegs be? Point is, always have a look at the second nicest room in the house. Where is Malandrino's cabin?"

"His cabin?"

"Or stateroom, as you prefer. I'm still learning the pirate patois," I said. "Malandrino did have a stateroom, I assume."

"He did, yes. He was the only performer who had his own room on board, in fact. Everyone else shared a dormitory below decks." The commodore reflected for a moment on this iniquity. "Would you like to see that?"

"I wouldn't want to bother the artists," I said. "If they're anything like theatre people they'll be just getting out of bed and in need of strong drink."

"There are no other performers at the moment, really.

They're meant to be joining the voyage at Saint Tropez."

"Then we've plenty of time. Let us begin with Malandrino's stateroom."

"Well, in point of fact, it's that door just there." The commodore gestured to the first cabin along the deck, between the barrel of gunpowder and the barrel of confetti. "It's not much to look at though, really, just a sort of stateroom. More of a cabin, really."

"All the better."

"It's probably locked."

"One way to find out."

"Might be some of his private affairs about, you know — not really cricket."

"I doubt he'll object."

"No, no, I expect he won't." The commodore shifted and shyed. He tried his hands in his pockets and found the exercise wanting. He kneaded his fingers for a bit, instead, and then said, "Listen, Boisjoly, before we go in there, there's something you should know."

"You and Malandrino were acquainted before he was known as Malandrino the Magnificent, and there's something incriminating in that cabin."

"Why, that's uncanny." The commodore appeared to exhale a breath he'd been holding since breakfast. "How did you know?"

"I didn't," I admitted. "But it was either that or that room is where you keep your collection of something mortally embarrassing. My second guess was a doll hospital."

"Malandrino's real name is Horndurfer. Rudyard Horndurfer." The commodore searched the empty deck for prying ears. "We called him Ruddy in the army, because he was rather famously, well, ruddy, if you'll forgive the language."

"Think nothing of it, Commodore," I assured him. "I was often witness, as a child, to my mother's bridge tournaments. I've heard it all. And I appreciate your candour."

"You'd have discovered it all soon enough." The

commodore led to Malandrino's stateroom door. "It's all in here." He opened the door and we stepped inside.

"Well, of course," said the commodore. The room was completely empty.

"Malandrino lived a spartan lifestyle," I observed. "Doubtless an imperative of the vagabond instinct to eschew the yoke of possessions, the lonesome liberty of the travelling circus."

"Everything's been taken," said the commodore. "He had all manner of private affair in here — clothes, photographs, souvenirs and, let us say, trophies — a big trunk full. Great leather and brass steamer trunk. It's gone, too."

The room was small and simple, as staterooms tend to be, and furnished with a single bed, a locker sort of affair, and a bureau with several drawers. The locker was open and empty, as were the drawers of the bureau. The only evidence that anyone had ever inhabited the room was hanging on a coat hook on the wall — a big brass ring.

"What were you anticipating, Commodore?" I asked.

"Scrapbook sort of affair, newspaper accounts, and the like, of the actions of our mounted brigade during the Action of El Mughar." The commodore wandered the room distractedly, looking behind and under furniture. "I commanded a small company of yeomen, at about the furthest edge of the offensive at Hulayqat. Our scout noticed a bit of an enemy blind spot that, taken in the instant by enough chaps on fast horses, would put us almost entirely at their back."

"Bravo, Commodore. I take it you survived."

"It all went quite well, yes." The commodore seemed to recall this with some surprise. "But as I say, we were the very fingertips of the operation, and if I was going to change strategy to exploit enemy error, HQ would have to be informed. I selected our best and quickest rider to carry the message."

"Ruddy Horndurfer."

"That's the chap. Even then he was an accomplished circus performer. Could ride a horse standing on his head — often did. He was the right man for the job."

"But he failed to deliver the message, I take it."

"Oh, no, he reported to HQ in double time and to excellent effect," said the commodore. "A machine-gun company returned and drew the enemy division into a distraction, and we rode them down from behind. A complete success."

"I'm not a military man, Commodore, so you'll forgive me if I miss some of the nuance, but from my civilian perspective, this all sounds like a result."

"T'is. T'was, I mean." The commodore nodded agreement. "And when it was all over, I reported it exactly as it transpired. Plenty of credit to go round, you know, and I confess I took some for myself — it was my snap judgement that took fortune at the flood, after all."

"But Ruddy had already told a different story," I surmised.

"He did, the ruddy... chap." The commodore cast about for something to glare at, and settled on the brass ring. "Before the action was even over, the papers had it that it was Ruddy that noticed the blind spot, then had to talk me into taking advantage of it — this was the most difficult part, to hear Ruddy tell it, owing in equal parts to my cowardice and blind deference for authority. Then he led us through, put us in position, and raced back to general quarters to apprise them of his heroism."

"I can guess the rest," I said. "The papers had their story, and had moved on to the next. Fleet Street, it is often said, goes only one way."

"No, well, nearly, not exactly," the commodore prevaricated. "That would have been better, in the end. Probably should have just left well enough alone. I tried to make my case, you see, but as mentioned Ruddy was already a minor celebrity before the war. After the Action of El Mughar, well, you can imagine. Practically beatified. My alternative account of the events were not given due consideration, to say the least."

"Ah," I sympathised.

"Yes." The commodore nodded gravely at the brass ring. "The papers worked up a quite elaborate profile of me as a jealous failure. Even got ahold of my old school reports."

"Oh dear."

"There was a cartoon in Times, depicting Ruddy as Henry V, and me as Falstaff."

"Biting."

"Remarkably good likeness, too, I'm sorry to say."

"And they so rarely are."

"And Penny Fairweather broke off our engagement." The commodore's tone was now that of one distantly musing on a classic of gothic fiction.

"How did you get on with Malandrino as a passenger? I asked.

"We didn't speak a great deal." The commodore looked to the ceiling and considered what he saw there. "It was he that brokered this arrangement with Digby. I suppose he may have been trying to make it up to me, for all the good it's done me." He regarded me straight, now, with a clear eye and frank aspect. "At any rate, Anty, I'm glad of the chance to say so — I'm not particularly sorry that Ruddy's dead. I'm just relieved there's no doubt that it was an accident."

"Ehm, well, in point of fact, Commodore..." I began, but in that instant the door swung open as though on a tether, and a muscular, minimalist moustache-stand appeared. In addition to a tightly curled, black W of a moustache, he had a curly black globe of hair, he was encased in a powder-blue léotard with a sequined starburst on the chest, and he carried two suitcases.

"What are you doing in my room?"

CHAPTER FIVE

The Bolder the Yodeller the Colder the Shoulder

"Anty Boisjoly, this is Norton Bean." The commodore introduced the acrobat.

"Beano," corrected Beano.

"Like the baked beans?" I asked.

"No," said Beano coolly. "Not like any baked beans. There is no such baked bean."

"Oh," I said. "All right, then."

"Is there?"

"Is there what? A baked bean called Beano?"

"Yes."

"Let me reflect…" I effected to do so. "Beano's a dream Oh! The best that's ever been Oh!" I allowed that to echo for a moment. "Yes, I believe there is."

"Then I am the Astounding Bounding Bean," declared The Astounding etc. "What are you doing in the room of the Astounding Bounding Bean?"

"This is Malandrino's room," said the commodore.

"Malandrino is dead." The A.B.B. stepped proprietarily into the room. "Crushed under the weight of obsolescence and desperation. Now The Astounding Bounding Bean is the headline act, and this is the stateroom of the Astounding Bounding Bean."

"Right, well, we'll leave you to it, Astounding," I said. "Doubtless you'll want to get started on making the house a home. Sure you don't want us to linger longer? We could help shelve your library."

"No."

"Quite sure? I read classics at Oxford," I said. "And a *Halfpenny Marvel* on the train to Portsmouth."

Astounding dropped his suitcases and crossed his arms. He appeared to wish to communicate something in this action, but I was stumped.

"Tell me, 'Stounders," I said. "Did you see Malandrino the night he died?"

The Bean nodded. "Of course. He was in the audience and, like everyone, struck dumb by the bounding of the Bean."

"You performed on board the yacht the night of the launch party?"

"I did. I perform because I must. I perform as Malandrino would have performed, if he hadn't allowed success to make of him a performer playing the role of a performer."

"I'm not sure I grasp the distinction," I admitted.

"No, it's subtle," allowed Astounding. "Call it a measure of commitment."

"Malandrino wasn't committed?"

"Dancing bears?" The Bean said this as though it was the circus equivalent of selling pencils. "Performing elephants? Why not chickens pecking tunes on bells? Or a flea circus?"

"I should mention, 'Stounds old bean, that I've never been to a circus," I said. "Are these bona fide examples of the wonders to be seen?"

"There was a time when Malandrino was true to the craft," continued Beans, while hefting his suitcases onto the bed. "His blind-folded, high-wire man-on-fire was, for me, an epiphany. His flying trapeze double-act — One Hundred Rings of Brass — was a symphony of synchronisation. Because of it, very briefly, even The Astounding Bounding Bean considered working with a partner. And I confess, his cloud of doves was poetry in flight, but that was the beginning of the end for

Malandrino, the first of his animal acts."

"You don't approve."

"I find it cheapens the art." The Bean opened a suitcase and removed a full-sized, signed, studio profile of The Astounding Bounding Bean from his 'Beano' days. He held it at arm's length against the wall over the bed.

"Did you happen to notice what time Malandrino left the yacht?" I asked.

"Precisely, no, I didn't." The Bean tried the picture now on the door. "But nevertheless I can tell you exactly when it was — it was the moment I finished my act. I could see it in his eyes — even before I juggled three unicycles while riding a unicycle — he knew his time had come. He must have raced off to his elephant with some new, desperate and, doubtless, risky addition to the act that he hoped would keep him ahead of The Astounding Bounding Bean. This rash hope killed him."

"Max Minefield believes something very similar," I said. "He thinks that Malandrino died trying to win his approval."

"That artless, pointless folderol? That self-satisfied, self-aggrandising grave-robber?"

"You've met?"

"Do you know what he said about me?"

"Not verbatim, no," I said, "but I'll bet it was along the lines of, if it hadn't been for your thingamy, he'd have thought he was at a whatsit."

"'Had it not been for Beano's almost superhuman lack of charisma, I might have believed I was at a circus.'"

"Must have been an early effort."

"Hold this." The Bean invited me to position his portrait between the portal windows so he could view it from a distance. "Minefield attempts to build his tawdry reputation on the rubble of careers he destroys. He's a vandal whose fame is that he has carved his initials onto a Michelangelo."

"Was he at the launch party?" I asked.

"I did not notice," claimed the Bean, appraising his portrait. "Try it higher."

"Minefield was there," said the commodore.

"With his back to the performance," added the Bean. "Looking off the starboard side, towards the setting sun, asking what time the fireworks were going to start."

"Did you notice when he left?"

"Certainly after the fireworks," said the commodore. "Everyone stayed for the fireworks, except Malandrino."

"Would you have known that for sure?" I asked, slowly losing my strength. "I'm going to have to put this down quite soon, Bean old bean."

"Everyone was gathered on the bow," said the commodore. "As you saw, there's too much equipment for anyone to be anywhere else."

"Intriguing," I said. "Hold this, Commodore."

The commodore assumed my gallery curator duties. "What's intriguing about it?"

"Minefield was on the starboard side, watching the sun set, as is convention, in the west," I recalled.

"So?"

"The boat is anchored to the east of the island. So, why didn't anyone see Malandrino's boat going back to shore?"

"Oh, I say, that rather narrows it down," said the commodore. "He must have left either during the show, or during the fireworks."

"Well, that hardly narrows it down," I said.

"No, I suppose it doesn't at that," agreed the commodore. "It was dashed dark by the time the fireworks started. Couldn't see the difference between land and sea. And of course during the performance all eyes were on Beano."

"The Astounding Bounding Bean," corrected Beano.

"Just so." The commodore nodded gravely. "Can I put this down?"

"Yes." The Astounding Bean waved away the picture and withdrew a larger one from his luggage. This one was a reproduction of a broadside poster, featuring a likeness of Beano riding a unicycle and juggling butcher's knives. "Try this one."

The casino of the Riviera Royale has an elaborate, wrought-iron mezzanine that extends outside where it becomes an elaborate, wrought-iron awning and al-fresco dining room. The dividing line is a high, stained-glass doorway in the form of a storyboard depicting, in twelve panels and from the initial survey to hammering down the last spike, Victoria's personal involvement in bringing the railway to India.

Rémy led me to a big marble bistro table overlooking the marina and harbour and with a view of the moiling, boiling rapids between the rocky Riviera mainland and Cap Royale. The sun had dipped just below the top of the casino but still blazed on the foothills of the Alps and warmed the air to a temperature which doesn't really exist more than, say, twenty miles from the Cote d'Azur on a summer's evening.

"The menu most English, Anty." Rémy handed me a card the size of a summons, but with an encouragingly limited list of charges carefully hand printed in the very centre under the legend 'Menu Regina'.

I don't typically have a lot of space in my luggage for nostalgia when I travel — part of the point of going somewhere else is that things are different there. But the Riviera Royale kitchens had put together an irresistible menu of English classics like 'Steak and Sydney Pie', 'Indian Games Hen', and 'Roast Carvery with Yorkfish Pudding'.

I was trying to determine if I had the appetite for a full serving of 'Suit Stue' when I happened to let my eyes fall on the marina square, and spotted Aunt Jacqueline taking her daughter's side in the controversial fraternising with croupiers debate. She was very publicly and playfully dining with a chap I recognised as the roulette wheel operator from the previous evening. And why not? I expect he had a lot of amusing stories to tell. He appeared to be telling one now, in fact, and Jacqueline was giving him one of those 'oh, you' shoulder shoves that guests of five-star hotels famously never give the staff.

"You're here already, Anty dear," said Mama as she breezed through the stained-glass ode to the fantasy queen. "I arrived late. I naturally assumed you'd still be in bed. It was darling of you to get up so early just to have dinner with your mother."

I rose and kissed the maternal cheek. "In point of fact, Mama, I was up with the noon cannon."

"Then how did you manage to stay out of the sun? You're paler than when you arrived. Practically transparent."

"Straw boater," I explained. "Vickers says that I have a noble complexion."

"Vickers? Rupert Vickers? Your father's old valet?"

"That's the chappy. My valet now. I rescued him from ignoble footman's duty after you drove him into the snow."

"I assumed you'd have pensioned him." Mama took up the menu and effected to be distracted by it.

"I assumed that you had pensioned him," I replied. "Why didn't you?"

"Because I have no money, Anty — your dear father left practically everything to you."

"Did he?" I marvelled. "Then what are you living on?"

"I have the Quillfeather trust fund, of course. That's ten thousand a year."

"Is that a lot of money?"

"I won't need to sell any jewellery any time soon." Mama put her hand instinctively to her diamond necklace worth, I would conservatively estimate, a pile.

"Papa gave you that for your tenth anniversary, if memory serves," I recalled. "Had it specially made by Aspinall's. Came in a big mahogany box with a brass plaque — there was something quite memorable about the inscription…"

"He misspelt my name."

"Not really."

"With love on our tenth anniversary, from Edmund to my darling wife, Cleopastra," recited Mama.

"Might have been Aspinall's mistake."

"He wrote it that way on the card, too."

"Now I think back," I said, thinking back. "Didn't he

sometimes pronounce it that way?"

"Quite often," confirmed Mama absently. "Mainly after seven o'clock, though, when I'd stopped listening."

"Probably an initial slip of the tongue that he wouldn't let go. You know how proud he was."

"Do I?"

"Well, I certainly do," I said. "Do you remember when he took to yodelling?"

"He was proud of his yodelling?"

"Not as such, no. At least, if he was, it was for its hidden qualities. No, he took up yodelling to account for the commercial quantity of throat pastilles that he ordered from the continent, because he was led to understand that they were of a sort that hide the external effects of drink."

"Did they?"

"Not in any way discernable to anyone with working senses," I said. "If anything, they compounded the problem — I think he saw them as a sort of immunity pill, as the armour of Achilles was so tragically worn by Petroclus. Do you really not recall this?"

"Your father yodelling?"

"Yes, my father yodelling."

"It never captured my attention."

"He was very committed to the ruse. He spent three months in Appenzell, perfecting the craft, just to add verisimilitude to the scheme. Came back with a beard."

"I do recall a bearded fellow who stayed with us for a month in '22."

"That's the chap."

Rémy seemed to pop into existence next to the table with a tray and two tall glasses of dark fizz and crushed ice, and a slice of cucumber clinging to the side.

"The Pimm's Cup," announced Rémy as he craned the drinks into reach. "You have chosen your dishware?"

"Tempted by the Brief Wellington," I said. "Mama?"

"It's very nice." Mama spoke a bit cagily, even for her, and aimed a wily eyebrow at the hotel manager. "Perhaps a trifle unconventional, but very nice." She handed Rémy her menu. "Scotch Cuddles for me, please, Rémy."

"Malandrino was murdered," I said, after Rémy had completed the inquiry and gone off to make his findings known to the kitchen.

"Then you agree with Deebee that an elephant can be guilty of murder."

"On the larger legal point I reserve judgement," I said. "However with respect to this particular elephant, no, I don't. Whatever the manner of death, Malandrino was murdered by human intervention. You're quite sure you didn't see him on the yacht the night of the party?"

"I believe that I have already addressed this question, Anty."

"Right oh." I drew meditatively on my Pimm's Cup, which is normally a refreshing, cool, summer drink. And so was this, whatever it was. "What is this?"

"The Riviera Royale takes enormous pains to reproduce the British summer, but they always get something charmingly and locally wrong," explained Mama. "That's a Pimm's Royale, with champagne, but they don't keep any Pimm's on hand. It's coloured nicely, though, with regional produce."

"Some sort of liqueur, is it?"

"Squid ink."

"Oh, well, close enough." I drew more inspiration from the ink drink. "What *did* you see?"

"Fireworks."

"I was referring to Minefield, for example, and the biddies. I spoke to them, by the way — did you know that they both carried a torch for Malandrino?"

"So I understand. They were two of his countless entanglements from his youth. Two that rather lingered."

As it happens, in that moment the biddies arrived on the terrace. They gave us chipper, smiling waves as Rémy led them to a table in the shade.

"Then how is it that they're such good friends?" I asked.

"Routine, I think," speculated Mama. "They've both been preoccupied with Malandrino — and keeping one another away from him — for so long, that it just made sense to start sharing expenses and travel arrangements. They probably long ago gave up on any hope of actually bagging him."

"Must have been an extraordinarily charismatic chap," I noted. "Was he?"

"I really couldn't say, Anty. I had very little to do with the man." Mama returned the biddies' inky toast from across the terrace. "Although it's certainly so that the biddies were hopelessly smitten. My understanding is the rivalry had taken a commercial turn — they were each trying to raise enough money to finance Malandrino in his own solo floating high-wire act."

"He was striking out on his own?"

"Not that I know of," said Mama. "I just know that's what the biddies thought, and they were competing to see who could give him the most money."

"Ah," I twigged. "I gathered that the late Malandrino may have been silently braving a debilitating scruple deficiency. The words 'alley cat' weren't explicitly spoken, but I could hear them purring in the subtext."

Scotch Cuddles, which I think started out taxonomically as collops — normally cross-cut beef or venison — turned out to be scallops coddled in butter and garlic. Brief Wellington was very near the original innovation of a fillet of beef baked in a crust, except it was salmon. Very toothsome, all around, particularly when paired with a chilled Cabernet Sauvignon Pale Ale.

We finished our rhubarb crumble (made with Sicilian lemon) and minced pie (served flambée) and Mama set out her traps at the baccarat table and I lingered on the mezzanine, contemplating the dizzying dance of destiny that is house rules gambling.

It was early yet, though, so apart from Mama installed at baccarat and receiving the first martyr to mathematics, there was only Max Minefield at the roulette table, across from Jacqueline and Chadwick. Max was in a black silk dinner jacket and the ladies were in plunging backless numbers, all brocade and feathers and perplexing pleats and gathers. The panicky little pearl had just clattered onto something black and the croupier — the one with whom Jacqueline had been fraternising on the port — added to what appeared to be an already towering stack of victories.

"Extraordinary woman, Jaqs." Deebee volleyed this view hard at the back of my head. The commodore and the circus mogul took places either side of me at the wrought-iron railing. "Got the Midas touch."

"Yes." The commodore nodded dumbly, as one mesmerised. "Uncanny luck."

"Much like my mother," I agreed. "Skips a generation, unfortunately, but I did get the Quillfeather vertigo, so it all balances out nicely."

"Eaten?" asked Deebee.

"Heartily," I replied. "I'd loosen my belt, were I not wearing braces."

"What's good? Or more to the pressure-point at hand, what's quick?"

"Carvery, typically," I said. "Although you'll want to approach it with an open-mind and, quite likely, a fish-knife. Do I understand you to be pressed for time?"

"Got to measure Little Miss Fortune's aft hatches," explained Deebee.

"Putting on a little vacation bulge, is she?"

"Getting her fitted for a new generator," clarified the commodore.

"Finest money can buy," added Deebee. "Coal-powered, twin-turbine, all-copper coils, graphite brushes. It's what Michaelangelo's David would be, if it were a generator."

"Does it do any tricks?" I asked. "You could put it in the show."

"Exactly what I'm going to do." Deebee rubbed his hands together, as though warming them on the flames of a burning orphanage. "Next week, judicial history will be made as, before a live, paying audience, Thumpy the elephant is put to death — by electrocution."

CHAPTER SIX

The Clown Found Ground and Renowned as an All-Round Hound

"You can't electrocute Thumpy," I protested.

Deebee rested his stresses on the mezzanine railing. "I wouldn't have thought so either, but the manufacturer stands by his generator. I have a written guarantee."

"It might interest you to know, Deebee, that I have sound reason to believe that Thumpy is innocent."

"You think someone else trampled Malandrino to death?"

"Not directly, no," I conceded. "I'm still turning certain key details over in my mind. For instance, the precise time that Malandrino the Magnificent left the yacht."

"I thought that was settled." Deebee looked to the commodore for support, and received it in the form of a firm nod. "Must have been during the fireworks."

"But you didn't see him."

"No one did, Anty," contended the commodore. "We were watching the fireworks."

"Exactly. How, then, do we know that he didn't leave much later? Everyone's alibi rests on the assumption that Malandrino was killed during the launch party, but there's absolutely nothing to prove that he didn't leave after everyone else."

53

"Apart from the boats," said the commodore.

"The what now?"

"The launches," clarified the commodore. "When the guests were gone there was only one left. It's the boat I used to come ashore in the morning."

"Yes, right, that's all very well and good, and largely in line with expectations," I claimed. "And it brings us nicely to what time everyone else left the boat."

"Extraordinary!" declared Deebee, who had lost interest and was watching Jacqueline rake in another stack of success. "How's that, Boisjoly?"

"Would you have even known what time everyone left?" I asked.

"I think so," ruminated Deebee. "Apart from Malandrino we were all on the bow, for most of the evening." Deebee turned his attention to Wairing. "Except you, Commodore, of course."

"No, no, I was right there with you all evening," said the commodore. "And you're quite right, everyone was gathered on the bow for seafood grill and fireworks."

"But for about ten minutes, I'd say, Commodore," persisted Deebee. "You remember, you were late lighting the fuses, and I said, 'What ho, Commodore, no way to run a circus.'"

"Oh, well, yes, of course, had to mind a spot of yacht business." The commodore spoke of 'yacht business' as though it was a broadly understood idiosyncrasy of life on the high seas. "No crew, you understand. Got to do everything myself, haven't I?"

"What about Max Minefield?" I asked.

"What about it?" Deebee asked back with a soupçon of disdain.

"Was he there the entire evening?"

"I think so." Deebee regarded the skylight and stroked his

chin. "Or was that the broken bilge pump?"

"He was there," said the commodore.

"He left with the other guests?"

"Yes." The acknowledgement appeared to cause Deebee some discomfort about the temples. "He was on the bow with everyone the entire evening. Although, hard to tell with his sort — I understand they can ride a moonbeam and turn into bats at will."

"Are you not fond of Mister Minefield?"

"You could say that." Deebee shared another certain nod with the commodore. "Man's a jellyfish."

"I'd have said barracuda," suggested the commodore.

"Barracuda's a tireless hunter," differed Deebee. "Works for what he gets. Minefield's a jellyfish, wobbling and waggling about, just below the surface, no plan nor purpose, other than to sting everything that his lazy, toxic tentacles happen to touch."

"He makes a good case," the commodore said to me. "Minefield's a jellyfish."

"I'm glad to have the cladistical question settled," I said. "I like to keep these things straight. Why is Minefield a jellyfish?"

"Who's to say?" wondered Deebee. "Probably something in his childhood. I doubt his mother had much to do with him, if he had one."

"After a show in Cassis…" The commodore held up an 'and that's not all' finger, "…which he was invited to watch from the yacht… he called Little Miss Fortune 'an excellent venue from which to observe the always delightful spectacle of incompetent seamanship.' Nearly cost me my insurance. It's up for renewal at the end of the month as it is."

"And that would have shut down the show," added Deebee. "And shutting down shows is Minefield's favourite pastime, even before poaching patsies for his gala money pit."

Once again, here were alluring allusions to Minefield's secret project. I masked my curiosity in measured terms, "I'll give you a hundred pounds to tell me what you're talking about."

"Ask him." Deebee sneered in the direction of Minefield, who glanced up at that moment and issued us a smug little wave.

"Hello, you ripe kidney." Deebee couldn't be heard at that distance, of course, but he waved back and smiled an elusive, enigmatic sort of smile — what I imagine the Mona Lisa would look like had da Vinci captured the very moment when she began transforming into a werewolf. "He'll be happy to tell you all about it. Good luck getting him to shut up, in fact, once you get him started. He even tried to recruit Malandrino, right out from under me."

"Had Malandrino any funds to invest?" I asked.

"Not a sausage." Deebee shook his head as one yielding to despair for the profligacy of the modern tumbler. "He had the three Gs of bad habits — girls, gambling, and getting fleeced by girls and gambling. Certainly went through a lot of money, though."

"Then what was Minefield proposing?"

"He wanted to hire Malandrino, of course."

"As what?"

"As what? What do you mean, as what?" asked Deebee. "The man trained bears to dance on a high wire — you think Deebee wanted him to paint his ceiling?"

"Now you mention it, I'd heard something about Malandrino striking out on his own," I recollected. "But I understood that there was nothing to it."

"There *is* nothing to it," Deebee assured me. "It's just a tale he told the biddies so they'd keep giving him money. Perfectly harmless and he'd never leave me — Malandrino and I started out in the big top before there was such a thing, just me and him and a mule that he'd taught to do sums. I gave him his first unicycle. He gave me my first knife-throwing scar. Want to see it?"

"Keenly," I said, before Deebee could remove his jacket. "But perhaps not in this holy place. So, there was no risk of

Malandrino the Magnificent joining forces with Minefield the Decidedly Not Very Much So?"

"Malandrino loathed Minefield." Deebee glanced sidelong back into the pit of the casino, where Max still sat at the roulette table, struggling to light his long-distance cigarette. "Called him a vandal."

"It's such a delight when a village rallies round a common cause" I said. "I think that's everyone, now. The Astounding Bounding Bean used that very word to describe Minefield."

"You mean Beano?"

"Events have taken a turn for the astounding," I said. "He's not the sort to let the grass grow. In any case, like Malandrino, the Bean regards Minefield as a vandal."

"They're both allergic to vermin. It's a family trait."

"What sort of trait now?"

"Oh, right, you wouldn't know," said Deebee. "Beano and Malandrino are brothers."

Deebee and the commodore left for a terrace meal just as the biddies came in from theirs.

"Good evening, Mister Boisjoly," harmonised Mimpley and Biddicomb.

"Evening, ladies. Off for a flutter? Don't tell her I said so, but I strongly advise against playing baccarat with my mother as bank. She's a known sharp, wanted in twelve counties. She once had to shoot her way off a Mississippi river boat."

"Oh, no, Mister Boisjoly," said Mimpley, gloved and scandalised fingers to her lips.

"You know we never gamble," added Biddicomb.

"Sound policy," I said. "She's my mother and I'm a loyal son, but the fact is she has agents everywhere. Indeed, it's her network of spies who tell me that you ladies were until recently in the market for a good thing. Were that still the case, I'd direct you to the notorious Max Minefield, who's offering attractive terms to ground-floor investors."

"Oh, yes, Mister Boisjoly," said Mimpley.

"We know all about that," confided Biddicomb.

"You do, do you?" I said. "Just to be sure we're talking about the same thing, though, what do you know about it?"

"We have no need to do business with the likes of Mister Minefield," said Mimpley in a confidential tone.

"Not that we would, anyway," backfilled Biddicomb.

"Nevertheless, it might help to talk about it."

"Just ask him about it…"

"…and he'll talk your ear off."

"But if I were you, Mister Boisjoly…"

"…I'd avoid Max Minefield like the plague he is."

"Frankly, Mister Boisjoly…" Mimpley leaned in closer, followed by Biddicomb. "…we've got our money in a sure thing."

Both ladies dropped their gaze to the casino floor and I followed them back to the roulette table. Minefield was still there, but so were Jacqueline and Chadwick. Jacqueline was again doubling her money, this time on red, and Chadwick was entertaining herself by spinning a coin on the edge of play, just as the croupier dropped the ball back into the works. She observed the coin for a moment, and then in a chaotic scramble the ladies selected their blacks and reds.

"A sure thing, you say." I studied the biddies' earnest, wide-eyed smiles. "Makes a change from topping up Malandrino's operating fund, I expect."

"Oh, dear." Mimpley returned her fingers to scandalised lip duty.

"You know about that, do you Mister Boisjoly?" asked Biddicomb.

"I got it from Mama," I explained. "Don't blame her, though, I dissolved her normally iron discretion with lashings of squid ink."

"He told us that he wanted to strike out on his own." Mimpley said this to a non-judgmental spot she'd found on the floor.

"We knew it wasn't true, though." Biddicomb gave the spot

the fuller picture.

"How do you know it wasn't true?"

"Well, quite simply…" Mimpley looked at me now.

"…we were never able to scrape together anywhere near enough."

"And before we could raise any more…"

"…he'd spent what we'd given him."

"If we're honest, we knew the truth all along…"

"…that we were just financing an iniquitous lifestyle."

"Then, if it's not peering too far into the back of the bottom-right dresser drawer, why did you?"

The biddies shared a cheeky, unspoken reflection.

"He was just so very…"

"…very charming."

"Oh, do come along, ladies," I chided. "Even I'm not that charming, and I once convinced the membership committee of the Juniper — that's my club, you understand — to reconsider the application of Tipples Tiptree after two false accusations of bigamy. Fatally, it was before the nine legitimate accusations came to light, but charm can only go so far. Or I would have thought."

"I don't suppose it matters now." Mimpley once again thought to include the spot on the floor in the conversation.

"On the bright side, your future fund-raising enterprises can be entirely in aid of motorcycle racing or whip-and-top or whatever it is your generation is getting up to these days. Absinthe, is it?"

"All we know is the circus," complained Biddicomb to Mimpley, who nodded in grave accord.

"I'm green with envy," I admitted. "Should your sure thing somehow not work out, you know that the waters around the island are thick with sunken treasure."

"Really?" both the biddies bade.

"Oh, yes. It's said that without the layers of gold coins and rubied crowns the port would be six fathoms deeper — the consequence of action and accident during the age of tall ships, so my man Vickers tells me, and I think there's a roughly even chance he was an eye-witness. Are you strong swimmers?"

"I don't know…"

"…I suppose so."

"Was Malandrino?"

"What do you mean?" asked Biddicomb.

"Put another way, could he have swum ashore on the night he died?"

"Oh, dear, no, Mister Boisjoly," insisted Mimpley.

"No one could have," persisted Biddicomb. "You couldn't even see the shore, it was so dark."

"Assuming he left the yacht after dark," I pointed out. "No one seems to be able to say exactly when Malandrino was last seen on board."

The biddies compared worried countenances.

"It was certainly after dark," vouched Mimpley.

"But why would he swim to shore?" asked Biddicomb.

"I was hoping you might take a crack at that," I confessed. "The best I have is that he swam ashore as a minor component of an elaborate plan to complicate my life."

"I don't see how…"

"It's part of a process. Difficult to explain, at these early stages. It was like that for Einstein in the formative phase of Special Relativity — for years the section on the maximum speed of light was annotated with 'you're going to have to trust me on this.' In any case, the commodore's sure that Malandrino took a boat but, of course, he didn't see him leave."

"No, he was missing just before the fireworks started."

"So I understand," I said. "But neither Minefield nor Digby can say when Malandrino left the yacht either."

"Well, of course…" Biddicomb nodded, wide-eyed.

"…they were absent too," added Mimpley.

"Absent? As in, they were missing from the bow of the ship, or lost in each others' eyes?"

"Missing," agreed the biddies simultaneously.

"This is an unanticipated chutney among the marmalades," I said. "So, sometime between nightfall and the fireworks display, the only people on the bow were you two, Mama, Aunt Jacqueline and Chadwick, and the Astounding Bounding Bean."

"Oh, no, Mister Boisjoly," Mimpley seemed unusually distressed by my casual census.

"Beano had retired below decks before the fireworks," explained Biddicomb.

"I suppose this goes some way to explaining why no one will commit to when they saw Malandrino leave the boat — nobody did. Jacqueline and Chadwick are inexplicably vague and Mama barely recognised Malandrino. Do you know what would be tremendously helpful about now, ladies?"

"Do tell, Mister Boisjoly…"

"…what can we do?"

"You can tell me whatever it is that you're hiding."

"Hiding?"

"What could we possibly be hiding?"

"Come come, ladies, by your own admission you were both obsessed with Malandrino the Magnificent, and yet you claim that you took no notice of his activities all evening. Jacqueline and Chadwick are the same, speaking as though the bow of the yacht that night was overwhelmed with indistinguishable clowns. It's clear that some dark secret, perhaps the key to everything that happened, is being held back from me. It's not in my nature to resort to extremes, ladies, but you leave me little choice — speak up, or I shall tell Mama."

Once again the biddies mirrored studies in fret, which they then aimed at me.

"But, your mother…"

"She wasn't there either, Mister Boisjoly."

"She was with Malandrino…"

"…in his stateroom.

CHAPTER SEVEN

Baffling Business
on the Bustling Bow

"You know I always pride myself on my nose for the subtle ingredient, Vickers," I said to the aforementioned valet over a simmering cup of summer, from the cascades of a sea of bedsheets.

"You have a most uncanny facility, sir," agreed Vickers, distracted slightly by, in the one hand, a marine-and-white striped blazer and, in the other, a spat.

"This tea, for instance." I held up the cup for inspection. "Obviously locally influenced, with infusion of lavender and cactus flower."

"The kitchen of the Riviera Royale has a decidedly Mediterranean disposition."

"I'm also getting mint and marjoram," I continued. "Oh, and you've made it with seawater."

"Oh, dear."

"No matter. The orange juice, while mango, is delicious, and the Balmoral scones, the base of which is *farine de pois chiche* and the raisins in which are black olives, make for a refreshing change of pace. Incidentally, Vickers, Is there a baked bean called Beano?"

"Not to my knowledge, sir, no," Vickers returned the spat to its drawer and traded it for a different spat, "but it's not an item that we keep in current inventory."

"Well, if you ever hear tell of one, I came up with a corker of a jingle for it."

"I'll keep a keen note of it, sir."

The Riviera weather, having had such a widely acclaimed success the previous day, went with roughly the same programme for this morning. Beyond my panoramic windows a sky-blue sea met a sea-blue sky and both profited from the association. The sun found a spot it liked — just above and to the left of my terrace balcony — and occupied it with calm confidence.

Gulls offered colour commentary and a gentle woosh indicated warm relations between the palm trees in the square and a soft sea breeze. Presently, the noon-day cannon contributed its prima donna performance and gave the whole production a touch of Tchaikovsky.

"Have I overslept again, Vickers?"

"No, sir, that is the noon cannon."

"I mean to say, have I missed breakfast?" I clarified. "I was meant to have a bit of a reckoning with Mama this morning."

"I understood that you had postponed the discussion of your father's passing."

"Different reckoning," I said. "Different murder altogether, in fact. Indeed, business is terribly backed up these days — I think I know now why those City banking types are always complaining they've never enough time to nail down a decent debenture, what with the endless parade of arbitrage and asset consolidation. In all fairness, though, they're probably not still having their seawater tea in bed when the noon-day cannon fires."

"You refer, then, to the suspicious death of Malandrino the Magnificent," conjectured Vickers as he withdrew my tea tray.

"Magnificent seems a pale understatement, if half what I've learned of the man is true." I swam to the banks of my bed and padded to the bathroom, leaving Vickers to squire the daily armour while I analysed the bathwater. Much of the ensuing conversation was carried out *voce forte* through the bathroom door. "His charm was legendary, they say, and in some aspects more magnetic than my own. Of course, the man had the dubious advantage of being an unrepentant bounder, so, apples to oranges."

I submerged the upper decks to swab out the suds and seized upon the opportunity to briefly pretend that I was a shark. When I resurfaced, it was to Vickers saying what I thought was "...Mister Boisjoly."

"Yes?" I replied.

"Indeed, sir."

"Indeed what?"

"I mean so say," said Vickers with the tone of one who thinks he's clearing things up, "the entire staff."

"Oh, right oh." I alighted tubside and was absorbed into a dressing gown that outweighed me by about a stone. "Talking of the staff, have you had a chance to apply the cold hard light of Vickers? Spot any rogues that belong in the gallery? Because, as it stands right now, everyone with a motive to murder Malandrino was, ostensibly, on the yacht when he died."

Vickers stood in silent, staring awe. I'd seen this before, most recently only last week, as we prepared for travel. I'd left Vickers in my room in the morning, packing the trunks, and set off for the club, making a point of saying that I wouldn't be back until tea time. Once on the street, of course, I realised that I'd forgotten some vital bit of haberdashery — a flask, probably — and returned to my room. Vickers, on clapping eyes on me, reproduced the stunned countenance he now displayed, and said "I beg your pardon, sir, I must have dozed off."

"I regret, sir, that I'm suffering a severe lapse of recall." Vickers looked down at the tea tray in his hands, as though wondering how it got there and what it was. "I imagined that I had just now said that Mister Beaujolais and the staff..."

"You were talking about Rémy." I came to the light. "Of course, Vickers. You probably said exactly what you recall saying, but I was, during a brief but critical period, a shark. Could we do another take?"

"It appears that those who attended the party constituted the entire hotel guest list," repeated Vickers. "And this opportunity was seized upon to stage a full staff party, held in the casino, including Mister Rémy Beaujolais."

"So the entire hotel staff can alibi each other," I surmised and managed to simultaneously pull on boating trousers.

"Exactly, sir. The party lasted until the early hours. Furthermore, there is no one among the staff who appears to have had any connection with Malandrino."

"This is largely as expected." I finished buttoning the shirt and opened a clear path for Vickers to knot my tie. "All above reproach, I take it. Souls blanched clean by the steadfast southern sun and lack of want and hunger?"

"I don't know that I'd extend to that, sir." Vickers stepped back to review the tie, decided that it would do, and held my blazer in trawling position. "The maids and serving personnel seem quite sound, but there are some doubtful characters among the casino staff."

"Sleepy-eyed chap that permanently appears to be trying to remember how to smile, and a conically-shaped cove with a combover that looks like it's being loomed?"

"Messrs Turbie and Roquebrune," completed Vickers. "They're croupiers."

"And they strike you as a bit dodgy, do they?" I asked. "Me too. Can't put my finger on any one thing, but I don't like the way this Turbie bloke holds towels. Something very shifty about it."

"Monsieur Turbie offered to sell me a silver cigarette case that had been left behind by a previous guest," said Vickers. "And Monsieur Roquebrune suggested that I could make myself a tidy sum if I were willing to retrieve a package from Corsica."

"Whatever they're offering, Vickers, I'll double it. I need you by my side."

"Very good, sir."

"The situation is rather dire." I was pacing the room, now, and stopped at the open balcony doors. "Malandrino was definitely on the yacht up to and a little past nightfall. I'll get to the 'a little past' momentarily, and you'll be glad you waited. Everyone was gathered on the bow for, first, a display of acrobatics by a tumbler who turns out to be Malandrino's brother, and then a fireworks show."

"Yes." Vickers stepped out onto the balcony and I followed. He looked towards the yacht. "The casino party, I'm told, changed venue then, so that the staff could watch the fireworks. Alas, they were too late."

"Or too early. I understand there was some delay in getting started."

"Quite possibly. In either case, in the absence of a light show, the party moved to the point for a midnight bathe."

"Really?" I surveyed the point from the elevated advantage of the balcony. "That's intriguing. So anyone crossing the island from the marina to the beach would have passed them on the path."

"This seems a reasonable conjecture sir, yes."

"Well, now we're getting somewhere." I stopped short of snapping my fingers and, as it turned out on reflection, that was for the best. "Actually, that's much worse. It means that literally everyone, staff and guests, were accounted for when Malandrino died. Unless they saw someone. Did they see someone?"

"I fear not."

"Then the only possible explanation is that, somehow and for some reason, Malandrino met someone after everyone had come ashore, and that person somehow caused Thumpy to trample Malandrino to death."

Vickers cleared his throat with the subtle yet meaningful hem of the lifelong valet.

"You ahemmed, Vickers?"

"I did, sir. I'm afraid that this is an unlikely unfolding of events." Vickers ventured towards the edge of the balcony. "At an appointed time, the staff went to the marina to meet the skiffs returning guests from the yacht. It was a moonless night and extremely dark, I'm told, and it's customary on such occasions to chaperone guests with railway lamps."

"After which, presumably, they tucked them into bed, and locked them in."

"Not as such, no sir, but the effect is very much the same. Monsieur Rémy remained on night duty at the desk, and contends that he would have seen anyone leave the hotel."

"Of course he does." I looked upon the horizon for inspiration and the horizon, as it will so often do, just sat there. "You realise what this means, don't you?"

"That Thumpy the elephant killed Malandrino?"

"Of course not, Vickers," I said. "He wouldn't hurt a mouse. More likely to do himself an injury escaping one. No, I mean to say that what we have constitutes a locked room mystery, or as near as one can get on a tropical island. With the exception of the mysterious Jacqueline and her delightful daughter, Chadwick, everyone had history with Malandrino and everyone had cause to kill him."

"Surely not Mrs Boisjoly."

"And why not?" I asked. "This is the same woman who left me at Eton over Christmas because, she claimed, my room was being painted. This is the woman, you'll recall, who stopped your pay for two weeks to cover the cost of a broken Limoges music box."

"In her defence, sir, it *was* you who filled it with sand."

"And made the world a better place, but the principal remains," I contended. "And I conclude my indictment with our strong and shared suspicion that this is the woman who paid someone my father's money to push him under an electric tram at Wormwood Scrubs."

"Nevertheless," Vickers spoke with an uncharacteristic abstraction, and appeared to study the vast open sea. "I strain to reconcile the crime with the criminal."

"As do I, if I'm honest," I confessed. "It's difficult to imagine Mama tricking an elephant into trampling a clown. I could see her browbeating Thumpy into all manner of mischief short of that, but I can't bring myself to believe that she committed this *particular* murder, which leaves us spinning what Shakespeare would call Giddy Fortune's furious fickle wheel, if he had a mother like mine."

"Sir?"

"I have eye-witness testimony — rather unimpeachably obsessive eye-witness testimony, to anticipate a point — that suggests that Mama was the last person to see Malandrino alive," I explained. "And in circumstances that might also suggest a motive for murder."

"Very good, sir." This was barely disguised code for 'that will do.' Vickers maintains a firmly feudal sense of that which is and that which is not an appropriate course of conversation with a servant when talk turns to scandal among the quality, and he draws the line at 1860, give or take.

I steered onto the safe and sturdy ground of logistics. "In any case, like everyone else, Mama was on the yacht for the fireworks. Now, no one could have left that yacht, at least not for very long, but I can't help but be spellbound by the strange and overlapping absences from the party on the bow."

"Absences?"

"Of the strangely overlapping variety, yes," I confirmed. "Starting at roughly sundown and continuing until the fireworks started, in chronological order, Commodore Wairing disappeared. This was avowed by Deebee Digby, who neglected to mention that he, too, wandered off on his own, followed shortly after by Max Minefield."

"I think that I may have misheard, sir."

"No, you didn't. There is, among the suspects, one Max Minefield, circus critic."

"Again, sir, I fear…"

"And again, no, you heard right — circus critic," I confirmed. "Almost universally disliked. I say 'almost' because there are some on the island who have yet to meet him. I find him strangely intriguing, personally, not least because Mama won't let me near him — probably the same reason that the wine cellar held for me such a magnetic appeal as a child. Minefield has some secret project the success of which requires only the indulgence of a visionary with means and naiveté."

"Curious."

"Extremely, but no one will tell me what it is. Not even the biddies, who have proved themselves otherwise invaluable informants. These are the two devotees of the late, magnificent Malandrino who provided such a telling account of the events on the yacht, including a disclosure that appears at first glance to torpedo from close range Mama's contention that she didn't know the deceased."

"Could their views be clouded by jealousy?"

"I see what you mean." I regarded Vickers socratically. "They might be reporting through the selective magnification of the lime-green lens of envy. As it happens, I have yet to interview Aunt Jacqueline and Chadwick on the point. I believe that I shall focus my attentions on the younger. She strikes me as the more becoming."

"Sir?"

"Forthcoming," I amended. "I meant to say forthcoming. She and her mother were on the yacht and claimed to have not recognised Malandrino, which seemed reasonable at the time, when I thought that the deck was teeming with clowns."

"Strangely evasive," observed Vickers.

"Like an eel with a guilty secret," I agreed. "Nevertheless, we know that they, like everyone else, were on the yacht, because of the inventory of skiffs. We agree that no one could have swum ashore?"

"In the darkness and currents it would have been impossible."

"As I thought." I surveyed the swirling tides as they passed between the marina and the yacht and followed them to the point of the island. There stood the biddies, also watching the currents. "Incidentally, how much sunken treasure do you suppose there is in these waters?"

"I would have thought none at all," estimated Vickers. "The waters are very shallow, and anything worth salvaging would have been so years ago. Might one ask…"

"Oh, just a little thing I evidently invented as a segué to the question of swimming ashore," I explained. "A theory which you've rather deftly knocked over the head with the spanner of local knowledge, once again leaving everyone on the yacht during the murder."

"Everyone but the elephant," Vickers reminded me.

"Who is innocent."

"Just as you say, sir."

"You know, I've known you for slightly longer than I've known myself," I pointed out. "I speak fluent Vickers, and I can immediately detect the distinction between 'just as you *say,* sir' and 'just as *you* say, sir'. You think I'm a syrupy sentimentalist with a soft creamy centre, guided by first impressions and faith."

"Just as you say, sir."

"And you're right, I am. I've never met a sad-eyed elephant I didn't take to immediately," I admitted. "But I admire your cold-blooded if somewhat hard-hearted objectivity, Vickers, and so I present to you the evidence of the lock."

"The lock, sir?"

"The lock, sir," I affirmed. "It fell on the commodore's foot."

"I see."

"It fell on the commodore's foot, Vickers, when he unlocked Thumpy's cage the morning after the murder," I continued. "The lock in question is a heavy padlock, which seals the gate by a chain."

"And the lock was on the outside," twigged Vickers.

"Exactly. Someone locked Malandrino in."

Vickers nodded reflectively and gazed beyond the point. I had been watching the biddies but then my attention, too, was drawn out to sea. *Le fiable,* Pilque's fishing and ferry boat, was turning slowly in the swirl. The sail was set but sagging, and Pilque was struggling to board his trawling net, which appeared to be quite happy where it was in the warm, welcome waters of the *Cote d'Azur.* Pilque was having none of that, though, and he took up his gaff and swung it backhand like a one-armed golfer — a particularly gifted one-armed golfer — and subdued his catch.

Then with both hands and fisherman's strength, Pilque hauled over the side of *le fiable* a leather and brass steamer trunk.

CHAPTER EIGHT

The Chaotic Continuity
of the Croupier Community

My mother was not at the casino.

She wasn't there when I first stopped in, soon after my debrief with Vickers, and she still wasn't there after a traditional breakfast of klippers (grilled squid) and a poked egg (actually, a poached egg, and quite a nice one, too).

I surveyed the casino floor from the vantage point of the mezzanine, where once again the biddies had installed themselves, with a little bistro table and full complement of the tools of tea between them. It was early afternoon so it was unsurprising that the gaming tables stood largely idle but for *vingt-et-un,* at which Chadwick sat in a trim blue and white dress of naval influence, her storm of golden hair tied into a blonde fountain with a trim of blue ribbon. She was laughing with charitable indulgence at something the croupier had said. Something quite dull and inappropriate, no doubt. Viewed from above like that, I was of course struck by the uncanny similarity of the state of affairs as they stood for Perseus, who saved Andromeda from the sea-monster Cetus, played here by Monsieur Turbie. I swooped down on the wings of Pegasus, played here by the wrought-iron staircase.

"What ho, Chadwick." I slid onto the chair next to her.

"Oh, what ho, Anty." Chadwick turned and hit me in the eye with a solid ivory smile.

I listed, badly, but was given a moment to recover when Turbie asked, *"Carte, monsieur?"*

"Oh, uhm."

"Go on, Anty," urged Chadwick. "The table's hot."

I risked a hundred francs and the dealer gave me a three and a two, and he gave Chadwick a queen and a three. He gave himself an ace.

"And cooling quickly," added Chadwick. "Did you kick a black cat into a mirror under a ladder on the way in? Anty, this is Monsieur Turbie. He's a croupier, now, but he used to be a prize-fighter, isn't that right Turbs?"

"Oui, madame."

"Oui, indeed," continued Chadwick. "Left the ring in '22 during a bout with Maxime 'Le Crime' Pointeclaire. Mother and I were there."

"He quit after a single defeat?"

"You don't follow, Anty, he literally left the ring. In the second round," explained Chadwick. "Le Crime had a right hook like The Flying Scotsman going through a tunnel. Poor Monsieur Turbie landed in the press box and immediately retired to casino life, didn't you?"

"Oui madame," confirmed Turbie. *"Une catastrophe."*

"Not entirely," differed Chadwick cheerfully. "We had a hundred thousand francs on Le Crime — oh, dear, I think Monsieur Turbie is only discovering this now. Sorry, Turbs. You've always been lucky for me."

"C'est un plaisir, madame." Turbie smiled sportingly and then turned a professional deadpan on me. *"Carte monsieur?"*

I agreed the transaction and Turbie gave me a five, and then another, and then a ten.

"Vingt-cinq, monsieur. Madame?"

"And why not?" Chadwick tapped her cards with a lazuli lacquered nail. Turbie flipped her a knave.

"Vingt-trois, madame," said Turbie with sincere remorse. *"Un nouveau jeu?"*

Chadwick considered this. She glanced around the empty

casino and up at the biddies who smiled down on us. She gave me a coy, conspiratorial smirk, and then withdrew from a little canvas purse, of all things, a tinted monocle. She fitted the lens in her right eye and examined the table, with particular focus on the discarded cards and those which could be seen in the shoe. Finally she looked at her small but not insubstantial columns of winnings.

"I don't think so." She returned the monocle to her purse. Then she looked at me. "Mother says to always quit while you're ahead. Mind you, she also says 'always be ahead', so it's never unerringly clear how to apply the rule, but as you've so kindly offered to show me your elephant, I suppose it would be rude to keep playing blackjack in the middle of the day. I can play cards anytime, but it's been oh, weeks, since I last saw a homicidal elephant. Up close, I mean."

I chose the path around the point because, mainly, it's the only way to get to Elephant Beach, but also because it afforded a certain scenic adjunct. The Boisjoly charm, it has been shown time and again, is effective under all conditions, but can only benefit from turquoise waters bubbling and babbling against rocky reefs, balmy, briny breezes, echoing gulls and swooning treetops, and a honeyed sun pouring down over it all in thick layers.

"I saw you swimming just there, yesterday." I gestured with a glance towards the gateway to the calmer waters of the point formed by the twin mushroom rocks.

"I saw you see me swim in the sea, Anty. You carried off the straw boater very smartly. Not everyone can. Most men end up looking like a carnival barker. You did, too, but more the reluctant sort of carnival barker that you get at a village fête."

"Just the impression I was aiming for. I note that you have your own towel caddy."

"Turbie?" said Chaddy. "He does hold a mean towel. Shoulder-height, draped but still, not waving it about like a flag as some chaps will do. I think it's his croupier training — steady hands."

"All the same," I brooded, "something about your croupier strikes me as very dodgy."

"He's hardly my croupier," corrected Chaddy. "He's everyone's croupier. A croupier for the ages."

"The croupier currently under appraisal, then. I find him very dodgy."

"Anty — he's a croupier."

This observation of the already established was actually a trenchant shorthand for a pertinent point — Turbie was a croupier and, therefore, almost certainly above reproach. Chadwick knew — and knew that I knew — that casino dealers as a class are the professional manifestation of Jekyll and Hyde. It's the simple extremes of the lifestyle, I expect. Working in a casino is comparable in a surprising number of ways to taking holy orders — there are very prescribed moral codes and dress codes, social and idiomatic codes, and codes of behaviour, and the slightest breach of any of the above can result in swift excommunication without recourse to appeal. Also they spend their working day doing rote maths.

Not working in a casino — meaning the time that croupiers spend away from the tables — is the precise opposite. It's by necessity a period of liberty and abandon, a continuous, sleepless maelstrom of laudanum and causeless shouting, punctuated by fist-fights.

In short, the common-or-garden European croupier is the most dangerous, scarred, tattooed, unpredictable and thoroughly trustworthy wedge of wight you could expect to encounter outside of something by Robert Louis Stevenson. They might resell 'found' property. They can definitely be counted on to put you onto a good thing smuggling contraband from Corsica. What they do not do, however and ever, is cheat the house.

We entered the emerald jungle like Hansel and Gretel and I diverted Chaddy by pointing out the three species of flora I could identify. Four, if she counted grass. Presently we arrived at the pebbly beach and the sad, still remnants of circus life — stacks of hay, barrows of melons, wagons of canvas and poles, and a cage full of lonely elephant.

Thumpy was stretching his trunk to its fullest extent, offering a stick of hay to a seagull perched high on the bars of his cage. With a scornful plaint, the bird flew away and Thumpy watched after it as it swerved around the cliffside out of sight. He dropped his trunk to the floor of his cage and swept it forlornly back and forth.

"What ho, Thumps," I called as we approached. He turned to us and seemed to shed two years of sorrow in a moment. His bedsheet ears perked like a Pekinese and he raised his trunk and horned a happy honk. He thumped over to the gate and put his trunk through the bars and, according to established tradition, knocked me sideways with a friendly wallop on the shoulder.

"Big, isn't he?" commented Chaddy.

"I thought so," I agreed. "But I confess I'm rather out of my depth. Thumpy might be a dwarf by elephant standards. You concur he's a large animal, then."

"Well, as elephants go, I'd guess about standard." Chaddy put her hands on her hips and levelled a critical squint on Thumpy. "Maybe a little thin. Shouldn't he have food of some sort?"

"The commodore's meant to feed him every morning," I said, but we were simultaneously noticing that Thumpy's trough was empty. "Perhaps he forgot."

"Or Thumpy's a nervous eater," proposed Chaddy. "My mother's like that, except with martinis. Why don't you fill that wheelbarrow with watermelons and we'll make a nice picnic out of it. Thumpy might like some too."

"With you in principle, Chads, but I'll point out that the cage is locked."

"I noticed that." Chaddy bent to examine the lock. "Well, one problem at a time. The first problem is that wheelbarrow is over there, if you follow my line of reasoning, while the watermelons are over there, in that wagon."

"Right oh." I draped the striped blazer over a horizontal bar of the cage and set off in search of provisions.

One would assume that loading watermelons from a wagon at about shoulder height into a wheelbarrow on a hot day on a shadeless beach would make jolly work, and it does, given the right company, but it's taxing labour. I think this is particularly true if your normal, day-to-day activities almost never include loading things from wagons onto wheelbarrows. The nearest I've come, in recent memory, is taking down the laundry last March, I think it was, when Vickers did himself a nerve injury and couldn't lower his arms for a day. Gives a chap the chance to think, though, and by the time I had a fully-laden wheelbarrow I also had an idea.

"I say, Chadwick," I called as I loaded the last melon. "What we want to do, I think, is smash these things up and push them through the bars. They look quite substantial, I know, but I've dropped one already and it cracked like an egg."

I took my position at the handles of the barrow and looked to Chadwick for her views on my proposition. She was drawing the chain from the gate.

"Little known fact," she said, dropping the chain to the ground, "the bigger the padlock, the easier it is to pick. That one's huge. I don't know why they bothered to make a key — it should just come with a knob."

Chadwick dragged the gate open with her full body weight and Thumpy waggled his ears in joyful anticipation. Then she stepped into the cage and communed with a much more gentle elephant trunk than that which I'd been offered.

"Okay, enough of that." Chadwick waved Thumpy back. "Give us a little room to ranch in."

Thumpy interpreted these gestures more broadly than intended; he turned twice on the spot, and then hopped up onto the giant ball and balanced himself there. Chaddy applauded and Thumpy trumpeted proudly and then, amazingly, he walked the ball, rolling it expertly beneath his enormous feet, across the floor of the cage. Then he did it backwards.

This went on for some time — Thumpy displaying his every trick and Chaddy applauding him to new heights of pride in a job well done. I don't for a single second suspect that Chadwick was drawing out the performance to avoid helping me load the trough with watermelons, shift an entire bale of hay, and top up the water tank — it just worked out that way.

Eventually, Thumpy exhausted his reserve of tricks or energy or exuberant vanity, and we had a welcome watermelon break.

"Get to London, much?" I asked, and checked it off the list. I know from bitter experience to get the matter settled early. It's nearly impossible to reconcile the notions of, on the one hand, a pretty young woman with wit and wisdom and even the minimum quota of zeal for life and, on the other, a distaste for London, but I've seen it happen. It's rare, it's tragic, but it happens.

"Not as often as I'd like," said Chaddy. Innings.

"You must come and see me in Kensington," I proposed. "Stay on a bit, if you like. Stay forever. We'll have to get married to stop the neighbours talking, but I understand it's a very streamlined procedure these days, and can be performed on an outpatient basis."

Chadwick mused on this, aided in the effort with an ambitious mouthful of melon that left a perfectly formed pink drop rolling slowly down her chin.

"I'll give it all due consideration, Anty." She dabbed her chin with something lacy and lucky from her purse. "In the meantime, you'll have to get the proposition past mother."

"Thinks I'm frivolous, does she?" I asked. "I get that rather a lot. You can tell her, if you think it'll help, that as recently as last March I brought in the laundry by myself."

"On the contrary. She thinks you're a dry stick. She says you probably belong to a gentlemen's club..."

"The Juniper," I provided. "One of the finest in London."

"...and that you've never jumped out of a plane."

"Hardly the measure of a man," I pointed out. "I have it on good authority that neither Benjamin Disraeli nor Admiral Lord Nelson ever jumped out of a plane."

"You'll want to take it up with your mother, too, I expect."

"She'll be thrilled," I assured her. "It wouldn't surprise me at all if Mama had arranged for us to meet."

"No, I don't think so." Chaddy looked into a glistening red bit of watermelon for guidance. "I don't think she even knew that she had a cousin Jacqueline until we descended on Cap Royale. Between you and me, Anty, she didn't seem tremendously happy to see us."

"Take no notice of Mama's lead-lined personality." I waved away the worry. "It's an act. You know she effected to forget my ninth birthday? We laughed about it, in the end. Or, I expect we will, if she ever remembers my birthday. But, brief intermission, I'm getting the impression that you haven't really yet spoken to my father's relict."

"Not very much, no."

"Not even on the night of the launch party? On the yacht?"

"Oh, ehm, let's see…" Chaddy popped an ambitious amount of melon into her mouth. "…mmmh mphm."

"Mmmh mphm yes, or mmmh mphm no?"

"Sort of a bit no-ish, I suppose. It was a mad party. Clowns, barbequed swordfish, fireworks…"

"Really?" I said. "Because the biddy dispatch has it that prior to the actual light show there was almost nobody remaining on the bow. In fact, just you and your mother, the biddies, and my mother. Is that roughly how you recall it?"

"It was very dark."

"The biddies could see you."

"Do you think we ought to refill Thumpy's water tank? He might get the vapours. Do you think elephants get the vapours? What do you suppose 'the vapours' are, anyway?"

"Chadwick," I said flatly. "If we're to be married, there can be no secrets between us… No, belay that order, there will definitely be some secrets between us… but in three days Deebee Digby means to execute Thumpy for a murder he didn't commit. I need to know everything that happened that night."

"Very well." Chaddy, who had been sitting in the wheelbarrow, tilted to her feet and stepped towards the water. "Walk with me, Anty, I don't wish the elephant to hear this. We saw your mother with Malandrino."

"With him? With him how?"

"Just talking."

"Well, nothing very sinister about talking."

"No."

"But that's not all, is it?"

"Not quite. They went off together."

"I see," I said. "Where did they go?"

"Malandrino's stateroom."

"Oh."

"Could have been nothing."

"That's true," I agreed. "She might have just wanted to get out of the night air."

"Yes, that's probably all it was. Except…

"Except?"

"They were arm-in-arm."

CHAPTER NINE

The Stagey Cryptic
of the Cagey Critic

"I did not forget your ninth birthday."

Mama made this risible contention from the depths of a broad-backed wicker balcony chair, giving her the air of a stone idol on loan to the Riviera from some Pacific island — one of those remote archipelago nations that esteem high eyebrows above all human features. Her balconies gave out on the east side of the hotel, overlooking the port and, just beyond, Little Miss Fortune. I stood at the writhing, wrought-iron rail and we each held tall, icy glasses of Pimm's Summer Squid.

"I didn't say that you forgot my birthday, Mama. I said that you acted exactly as if you had."

"Which is not true either, Anty. I wish you wouldn't say such things to people. If you'll recall, that was the occasion on which I presented you your first precious metal cufflinks. Platinum, I believe."

"Very close, Mama," I conceded. "But that was my twelfth birthday, they were silver, and they were from Vickers. They belonged to his father. "

"Are you quite sure?"

"I have them in my room, if you'd care to see them. They're engraved in commemoration of the coronation of George IV."

"Oh, that's right." Mama allowed the point, very nearly graciously, but then added, "I suppose your father gave you a snuff box or club membership or something equally appropriate."

"Flask," I provided. "He emptied it first, of course, but I think that was more from force of habit. In his defence, he thought I was turning eleven."

"He could certainly spare it."

"I'll say," I recalled with awe. "He used to hide them around the house like an industrious squirrel anticipating a hard winter and, like said squirrel, he only remembered the location of about one on five. It was only just before we left London that Vickers found a box of what we thought were Christmas ornaments — each one filled with a different eau de vie. The gift of the Magi was a particularly memorable calvados."

"He could be very imaginative when needed."

"Appreciably too much so for his own good," I said. "Do you know that he was convinced that you'd hired a private detective to monitor his movements?"

"I did nothing of the sort."

"No, I didn't think you had, but if you did the chap was a master of his trade. Papa saw him everywhere — he appeared as a doorman, a bobby on the beat, an honour guard on Pall Mall — he even managed to infiltrate the Whig Club, disguised as the man who feeds the piranha."

"At least it encouraged him to behave."

"Quite entirely the opposite," I said. "Papa took to slipping this fellow a pound or two wherever and whenever he saw him, so he thought that, whatever he got up to, a reliable confidant was reporting to you that his habits were retiring and blameless."

"Why are you telling me this now, Anty?" Mama lazed a pointedly distracted eye on the distant mountain range.

"Catching you up," I explained. "You'd have heard most of it if you'd stayed for the entire eulogy, plus the story of the occasion on which he managed to fall out of a cab and into the fountain on Trafalgar Square."

"I'm familiar with the incident."

"Ah, but if you'd stayed on at the funeral, you'd have learned what issued — he claimed to have done it on purpose and, to prove the point, repeated the feat every night for a week. Bookies were offering as much as nine-to-one when he finally missed."

"I had a train."

"I know. You had urgent business on the Riviera, which brings us neatly to the business at hand." I spoke dramatically, turned suddenly, and spilt my drink theatrically. "Was it circus business?"

"Of course not. What a thing to say." Mama maintained a cool, distracted air, like a marble bust of Athena thinking of something else.

"How long had you known Malandrino, Mama?"

"I didn't really."

"Yes, you made that patently false claim already," I recalled. "I took it in the same vein as your contention that you didn't see him on the yacht the night of the murder."

"I merely mean that I didn't know him well."

"Do you think that's an advisable line of defence, mother?" I asked. "You see, I know that you were alone with him in his stateroom."

"And what of it?"

"What of it?" I asked aghast. "You have gone native here in France, haven't you? I've seen this before, now I think of it. When Tollgate Longbridge got back from Le Touquet in the new year, he was wearing a beret. *And* he tried to kiss me on both cheeks. He was only there the weekend."

"There was nothing to it, Anty." Mama spoke with that firm insistence that, with her, is so indistinguishable from earnestness. "I was feeling unwell. He offered his cabin so I might lie down."

"First-hand accounts report that you were arm-in-arm."

"I may have taken his arm for support. I was light-headed with sea-sickness, the boat swayed so."

"Really, mother, it was anchored in deep waters." I gestured meaningfully toward the yacht in the harbour where it was, indeed, still securely fastened.

"Well it swayed, Anty, and I needed to lie down."

"Very well, Mama," I acquiesced. "According to the laws of probability you must have told me the truth at least once in my life, who's to say now is not that venerable occasion? I'll take it as read that you weren't immediately forthcoming because you wished to avoid this very confrontation."

"Precisely."

"And now we've put that ugly patch behind us, you can tell me what else happened that night."

"Nothing else happened."

"A clown died," I pointed out. "That happened. Perhaps in your bumper-to-bumper frenzy of baccarat and beach parties and bottomless barrels of Pimm's cup, murdered clowns are a hazard to shipping, but I think that this particular instance, what with the life of an innocent elephant at stake, merits comment."

"I mean that nothing happened about which you don't already know," corrected Mama. "Malandrino brought me to his stateroom and left me there. I didn't see him again. I returned to the bow perhaps fifteen minutes later in time for the beginning of the fireworks."

"Who was there then?"

"Everyone, I suppose." Mama glanced idly towards the bow of Little Miss Fortune, now devoid of passengers, pointing with a vaguely elephantine melancholy towards the open seas. "The biddies, Jacqueline and Chadwick, Minefield, Commodore Wairing, and Deebee."

"What about Beano?"

"The juggler with the unicycles? He was gone by then, I think."

"And then there was a fireworks show," I continued. "How long did that last?"

"It was interminable," complained Mama. "Somewhere between ten minutes and all night. I lost all sense of time after what seemed like the hundredth exploding starfish."

"And then everyone returned to the island by boat."

"Not everyone, no." Mama leaned back with her drink and her think. "The commodore and that Bean fellow must have stayed aboard. And of course I have no idea where Malandrino was at that point."

᠊᠊᠊᠊᠊᠊᠊᠊ ᠊᠊᠊᠊᠊᠊᠊᠊᠊᠊ ❧ ᠊᠊᠊᠊᠊᠊᠊᠊᠊᠊ ᠊᠊᠊᠊᠊᠊᠊᠊

I wandered down to the port to await the arrival of Pilque and his surprise catch of the day.

The sun-bleached tables of the sun-dappled square were all but abandoned, except for the island's loneliest and onliest circus critic.

"What ho, Max," I hailed as I took the liberty of the chair across from him. This was under the shade of a generous fig tree and home to, in addition to Minefield dressed in tropical tax-inspector-white, a glistening pitcher of coconut lager and a tray of glasses.

"Hullo, Anty…" Minefield struggled and puffed for a bit, as I'd caught him during the complex mechanics of lighting a cigarette at the end of a bamboo holder the length of a fishing rod. "…just the chap I wanted to see. Drink?"

"I will, Max, cheers very kindly."

Max poured a tall milky beer, slid it across the table and followed it so that he was leaning forward and leering at me.

"I was very much hoping to get a chance to discuss my proposition with you, Anty."

"And I've been very much looking forward to hearing about it, Max." This was the untreated truth. It was hardly the first thing I thought of as I rose and the last fleeting thought with which I drifted off to sleep, but whenever I considered Minefield's secret project it was with incandescent curiosity.

"Excellent." Minefield drew on his cigarette in a manner that looked painful. "Most excellent."

Then, as people tend to do when about to impart some secret, he looked around. Normally, this is a perfunctory formality, but as luck would have it Minefield's eye was drawn to the hotel, up the drainpipe to the second floor balcony, and to the distant but penetrating steel of my mother's glare.

"Ah." Minefield withdrew and tapped his cigarette idly against the back of a chair at an adjacent table. "Perhaps now is not the right moment. I believe strongly in the moment, Anty, don't you? If necessary, the moment must be orchestrated, and it must be flawless."

"Are you afraid of my mother?"

"Desperately."

"You have no cause for concern," I lied, I think, with *force majeure.* Witnesses and, for that matter, suspects, are far more forthcoming when put at their ease. Minefield was clearly bursting to tell me about his project and I, happily, was vertiginous with curiosity. "Mama has blown the all-clear."

"Oh? Oh, excellent, well, capital." Minefield performed an obsequious little wave for the balcony. "What has she told you?"

"Only that it's the sort of thing that would interest me."

"Really? She said that? Well, I'll confess I'm surprised, Anty, but she's right — it should interest you. It should interest you tremendously."

"It already does, Max."

Max beamed victoriously and took another long, hard pull on his cigarette.

"Blast, I think it's gone out. Can you tell from that end?"

"Maybe a bit of an ember," I said. "Op, no. It's gone."

Minefield reran the precise programme of lighting a cigarette through a straw. Finally, he coalesced into his chair and raised his bamboo wand like a beacon.

"The moment is right," he announced, "for *Trapezy Peasy.*"

"Oh, right, very clever. Some sort of device, is it, that brings the thrills and skills of the high wire into the gardens of the nation?"

"Ha. Delightful." Minefield smiled indulgently. "No, nothing so pedestrian. *Trapezy Peasy* is a revolutionary theatrical breakthrough — the world's first high wire musical."

"Not really."

"What's missing from musical theatre, Anty?"

"Oh, not much, I wouldn't have thought," I reflected. "I could stand a second intermission. Singing along does build up a thirst, sometimes."

"Exactly." Minefield stabbed at me with his cigarette stiletto. "Actual danger."

"That's true," I agreed. "I'm not sure that's an entirely bad thing, mind you, but I confess I've never seen any serious harm come to anyone during a musical, unless you count Georges Carpentier's turn as Count Saville in *Wherever Wanda Wanders.*"

"Danger, pathos, comedy, snappy tunes — *Trapezy Peasy* has it all... and more! It's a magic, tragic, romantic, musical high wire act. I wrote it all myself, of course."

"Of course."

"Alouette loves Mervello, and Mervello loves Alouette — the classic story — but she wants him to quit the high wire because it's too dangerous. But Mervello knows no other life, and so he tells Alouette that he owes the circus manager an enormous debt, and until it's paid he must perform and perform at his limits. And so Alouette takes on the guise of Fabula, a masked mistress of the high wire, so that she can help pay down Mervello's debts. Driven to greater and more daring extremes by the appearance of this new rival, Mervello performs the most perilous stunt in high wire history — and he plunges to his death."

"So, she's driven her lover to his death," I summarised. "This is a love story?"

"It has a happy ending"

"Does it? I think I missed it."

"It's implied. She becomes a very successful trapeze artist."

"You might want to beef up that angle," I suggested. "It's a little dark for the West End. What if Alouette reveals her identity and saves Mervello?"

"Absolutely not." Minefield waved away the revision as though it was an artistically impaired flying insect. "Naturally, Anty, as a ground-floor, majority investor, you'd have practically carte blanche — I want your ideas... I need them — but not a word of *Trapezy Peasey* can be changed."

"Right, fair enough."

"This is the tag line for the playbill; 'Love has no safety net'."

"Oh, right, that's... I suppose..."

"And neither does *Trapezy Peasy.*"

"That sounds irresponsibly dangerous."

"Thank you, I know." Minefield took a compensatory draw on his syringe. "Visualise it. Real acrobats soaring over the heads of the audience — no harnesses, no nets, no fear."

"No chance of it playing in any known West End theatre, either, I wouldn't think," I said. "Randomly murdering members of the audience has gone almost completely out of style, these days. Might play in Blackpool."

"Of course, Anty, we'll have to buy a theatre."

"Buy a theatre?"

"Or build one." Minefield nodded thoughtfully. "Probably for the best, in fact. Either way the ceiling will need to be a hundred and fifty feet high."

It's worth noting here, in case it's not widely known, that no one willingly invests in musical theatre. The entire West End of London is financed by the unwitting participation of old family money who think they're paying off their sons' gambling debts, or buying them out of ill-judged entanglements with chorus girls. The lads would be shipped off to the colonies in manacles if their families knew the shameful truth.

The nearest I've come was a couple of years back. Chap I knew from Oxford, Shuckers Clamtree, showed up at the flat in Mayfair, Brooklyn Bridged his way past Gillingham, my valet at the time, and cornered me in my own morning room. I hadn't clapped eyes on Shuckers since school and even then we weren't on particularly intimate terms — I doubt I'd seen the man soaking wet or arrested on more than a dozen occasions — yet there he was energetically reminiscing his way towards a bald-faced ear-bite for the ages.

Finally he got down to business, he'd written a musical — a guaranteed stink bomb called *Ow! My Eye!* — and had lost a backer not a week before opening night at Twickenham Pally. He needed a mere five hundred pounds to see the thing through, and he guaranteed to triple my money before even considering a West End run.

We'd been at school together and *noblesse oblige* and all that, but I dreaded holding a substantial stub owed by, of all things, a playwright. So, I bet Shuckers five hundred pounds that he could easily raise the money elsewhere and, when he failed to do so, I wrote him a cheque and regarded myself well clear of the affair. *Ow! My Eye!* closed the following weekend.

"That's a high ceiling," I noted for Minefield's benefit, because he didn't seem to know that.

"Non-negotiable, Anty." He looked up at a ceiling that was and always would be imaginary. "You see, *Trapezy Peasy* isn't just the future of the theatre — it's the future of the circus. Once audiences see what can be done with my genius and your money, the days of the mud-floored, mouldy-canvased big top will be at an end. The era of the travelling circus will be over."

"As will the notion of the circus critic."

"My work in that arena will be complete, anyway." Minefield smiled at this consummation, devoutly to be wished. "Pity about Malandrino, but I did what I could."

There was something in this apparent *non-sequitur* that struck me as distinctly and ominously *sequebatur*.

"Didn't you try to destroy his career?"

"Exactly," affirmed Minefield with something that might have been pride, had that not been wildly inappropriate. "It was for his own good — I assumed you understood that the role of Mervello was written for Malandrino. And like Mervello, he loved too well the big top, and in the end he had to die."

"He refused to join your show."

"He did," fumed Minefield, and blew thin reeds of smoke from his nose. "And after all I did for him. It's why we had words that night on the yacht. I was giving him his last chance — he either joins the cast of *Trapezy Peasy,* or I destroy his brother's career, instead, and cast him as Mervello."

"Was the Beano game?"

"He offered to teach me some sword-swallowing techniques," recalled Minefield. "But if I had tuppence for every time I've heard that…"

"So you spoke to them both that night."

"Briefly, yes."

"Do you recall when?"

Minefield sipped reflectively on his coconut beer and gazed out at Little Miss Fortune.

"Malandrino, when I first arrived on deck, I believe. The Beano just after his act, and before the fireworks."

"He was present for the fireworks?"

"No, actually, he stormed off after we spoke." Minefield pointed along the deck of the yacht with his cigarette holder. "I followed him but he nipped below decks."

"And didn't return."

"Not that I saw."

"And neither did you."

"Not for about ten minutes. I went exploring." The cigarette holder continued along the port side to the stern. "I thought I saw someone shifting some of the equipment, but it was tremendously dark by this point."

"Probably the commodore or Deebee."

"Weren't they on the bow? They were when I left."

"Not according to the biddies. It was just them and Jacqueline and Chadwick."

"Not your mother?" asked Minefield in a tone that, had it been a gesture, would have been a wink. "Not to worry, Anty. Ask anyone, Max Minefield is the very soul of discretion."

A jolly and welcome sploshing and sputtering drew our attention once again to the water. *Le fiable* pirouetted once or twice in a gentle whirlpool before bobbing into port with Pilque at the tiller, back straight and chin up, returning from the sea as might have Ahab, had he caught his white whale and had it been in the form of a leather steamer trunk with brass trim.

I made my excuses and drummed my heels along the white and weathered planks of the dock towards the mooring where Pilque was landing his catch. I arrived in time to assist in holding the beast down while Pilque put a pike to its jaws and pried them open.

The interior was an unsurprisingly damp but surprisingly well-preserved mass. The trunk must have remained partially air tight, which explained why it was close enough to the surface to be recovered by Pilque, and how it came to be that much of the contents were undamaged. There were clothes and shoes and a waterlogged book, there was the album that the commodore mentioned, and all of these were to be expected. What I didn't expect to see was something that I recognised.

I took up a mahogany box, about the size of a complete works of Shakespeare, excluding the sonnets. I opened it and of course it was empty, but on the inside of the cover was a brass plate with the inscription *"With love on our tenth anniversary, from Edmund to my darling wife, Cleopastra."*

CHAPTER TEN

The Net Sum of Jetsam

"Ah, Vickers, you're here," I said to Vickers, who was. He was standing on the credenza next to the balcony doors, holding a shoe in one hand and a bamboo whangee in the other. "Doesn't housekeeping do the dusting?"

"Not to a Kensington standard, sir, no." Vickers examined the shoe and then the stick. "I believe that I was pursuing a wasp."

The available evidence supported this conjecture. The tea things were on a tray on the vast marble dining table and in the sugar bowl a wasp was living a timeless moment of reckless gluttony.

"I'm fascinated by your novel approach to the hunt, Vickers — the wasp is down here."

"I suspect that luring me onto the credenza was a component of a larger strategy."

"Doubtless you're right. The devil grants his favoured species an unearthly cunning." I placed the lid on the sugar bowl. "We shall release him in due course, when he's had time to reflect on his sins. In the interim, have you near-term plans to return to sea level? I have need of your insights and the wisdom of centuries of Scottish science."

Carefully retracing his trail to the summit via a window seat, Vickers descended and set about deciphering the Chinese puzzle box that is our travelling store of whisky. Simultaneously, I laid out my treasures on the dining table.

"A most handsome case," opined Vickers, as he improved the layout with a glass of golden effervescence. "Aspinall's. 1908, I would have said."

"My mother's," I confirmed. "It was found in Malandrino's steamer trunk."

"I understand, sir."

"I don't, but let us set that aside for the moment. What can you do with this?" I referred to the sodden scrapbook resting in a puddle of its own making. "I daren't open it in this state."

Vickers bent and examined the object as though he was considering bidding on it. "Seawater, I assume, sir."

"Correct. Pilque caught it in his net and I bought it from him. The man has, incidentally, either very canny negotiating skills or an exaggerated idea of the value of wet leather."

"The album cannot be allowed to dry naturally." Vickers returned to the credenza and withdrew from the top drawer an electric iron. "The salt will erode the ink."

"Fancy you knowing that and what to do about it," I marvelled.

"It is an expertise acquired of necessity, owing to your father's repeated misfortunes with fountains and canals."

"Of course."

"It's not widely known, for instance, that below Greenwich the Thames becomes a marine environment." Vickers placed a napkin over the album and gently applied the iron. "I learned the utility of the iron — heated on the stove, in those days, but the principal is identical — from the gentleman's personal gentleman of Lord Hannibal-Pool, when his lordship and your father experienced a mishap while negotiating the footbridge to Isleworth Ait."

"There's a footbridge to Isleworth Ait?"

"No, sir, there is not. This was the nature of the mishap." Vickers raised the iron and tested the cover of the album with his finger. "Using a hot iron, I was able to recover seventy-five pounds and a promissory note from Lord Hannibal-Pool for 'a cutting riposte'."

"And what's the prognosis for this amorphous lump?"

"Indeterminate, for the moment. Your father's documents were rarely submerged for more than an hour, the exception being a night he spent in a rain barrel."

"Which already presents an intriguing question," I noted. "What was the trunk doing in the water? We agree that it's been there for some time."

"Several days, I would estimate."

"Obviously someone threw it overboard, but it's mostly just the usual sad and threadbare wardrobe of the professional entertainer. Nothing incriminating. And even if there was, why not just discard or destroy the incriminating thing?"

"Was the trunk locked, sir?"

"It was. Pilque opened it with an enormous hook on a pole. Like something the pope would use to open locked steamer trunks."

Vickers removed the napkin and gently opened the cover of the album. "As the trunk was locked, it seems probable that if someone wished to destroy something inside it, the best and only option was to throw it into the sea."

"Yes, I see your point. What's that, Vickers?"

"A photograph, sir." Vickers once again applied the napkin and iron trick, and then peeled the picture away from the page. "It appears to feature Prince Louis of Monaco and several dignitaries. And an automobile."

As obscure as that was, it was bang-on. There was the Riviera's second most dangerous baccarat virtuoso with, on the left, several dapper and dashing young men with matching moustaches selected for their aerodynamic qualities, and on the right a coterie of photogenic flappers, smiling at the camera in a manner that made smiling at cameras look like true and noble work. Behind the pose was the famous casino and, foreground, stood one of those impractical little racing cars — a Bugatti or Mazeratti or Manicotti or some such thing.

"That's the shark," I confirmed. "I can see his fangs glinting from here. I probably paid for that car, you know, Vickers."

"Yes, sir. The Grimaldi family has long enjoyed good fortune when the Boisjoly gentlemen are in Monaco."

"Not just me, then."

"No, sir. I was with your grandfather when Joseph Hobson Jagger famously broke the bank at Monte Carlo when he perceived that certain imperfections in the balance of the roulette wheels allowed him to predict and profit from probable outcomes. They say that the six hours your grandfather spent simultaneously playing *vingt-et-un* saved the principality from bankruptcy."

"He once told me there was a monument to him at Monte Carlo. I was never quite sure if I should believe him."

"A very handsome bust sir, in Carrara marble. It's in the casino gardens overlooking the sea."

Vickers had been gently treating subsequent pages in the album and revealing little of interest — playbills and postcards and promotional stills of Malandrino — but now he opened to a page with a thick envelope fixed to it. On the envelope was written 'Bidelia'. As Vickers peeled the envelope away from the page, it turned to reveal another, similar envelope. This one was labelled 'Myrtle'.

"The biddies," I observed. "I'll bet you I can tell you what's in those envelopes."

I would have lost that bet, as it happens. I assumed that these were letters from the biddies to Malandrino. They weren't. They were letters — dated in the future — that Malandrino intended to send to the biddies. They were identical and ingeniously generic — 'I kept your most recent letter by my pillow so that you might sing me to sleep, and call me to wake...', 'Did I detect a note of despair in your last missive? Never doubt my dear (Bidelia in envelope one, Myrtle in envelope two) that you'll always be my one and only...', 'For her sake, let us never tell (Myrtle in envelope one, Bidelia in envelope two) of our special bond.'

"What a frightful bounder," I said. "We can assume that these are future instalments of a serial that already holds a position of gullible, giggly, girlish secrecy between the biddies."

"Let us hope so, sir."

"Oh, right, yes, I see your point." I regarded the letters, now drying, through the last of my whisky and soda, now dying. "Hell's fury is already famously outclassed by one woman scorned all on her own. What's that now?"

Vickers had uncovered a smaller album within the larger — it was a leather portfolio of wax paper backing of newspaper articles.

"This first one appears to be an account of the Action of El Mughar," said Vickers.

"Recounting the ingenuity and bravery of one Lance-Corporal Rudyard Horndurfer," I educatedly guessed.

"Yes…" Vickers was momentarily distracted by the Action of El Mughar. "His actions appear… improbable."

"Almost pure fiction, according to the commodore," I said. "He was the commanding officer of Rudyard Horndurfer, known to his fellow yeomen as 'Ruddy' and to you and me as the Magnificent Malandrino. Apparently, he stole credit due his entire company for a successful battlefield manoeuvre."

"Most telling." Vickers turned the wax page and his eyes fell upon a cartoon of a heroic, broad-chested and crowned Malandrino, holding off the hun with one hand, delivering what looked to be an important map (helpfully labelled 'important map') to general headquarters with the other, and riding a horse, standing on the saddle. Meanwhile, an uncannily accurate merging of Falstaff and Commodore Wairing was given the paraphrase from Henry IV: 'If I fought not with fifty of them, I am a bunch of radish.'

"Possibly," I allowed, "but Wairing volunteered this rather understandable motive for murder well before I was likely to discover it for myself."

"Does the name Penelope Fairweather feature in the scandal?" asked Vickers, his eyes on the following page.

"Luckless, faithless Penny didn't have the mettle for a life as the wife of a failed career soldier, publicly humiliated as a coward and a liar, and so easily depicted as Falstaff. I expect that last one was the straw that did in the poor camel. She broke off their engagement."

"Yes, sir." Vickers placed a finger on the damp page. "The original announcement is here, just prior to the war, and the termination is announced — it is a much larger bulletin, and the language is very frank. And final."

"Poor chap."

"Indeed, sir. The second engagement is announced only days later."

"Second engagement?"

"Between Miss Penelope Fairweather and Mister Rudyard Horndurfer."

"This is new," I said. "I wonder why the commodore didn't mention that Malandrino married his sweetheart."

"Possibly because she did not," said Vickers, still reading. "There's a further announcement, six months later, informing friends and family that Miss Fairweather would be voyaging to Canada, to the port of Halifax, and onward to the province of Saskatchewan, where she will marry a wheat farmer some thirty-two years her senior."

"We learn many things," I mused. "Not the least surprising of which is that Saskatchewan is a real place. I thought it was something that Swift made up."

Vickers continued to perform surgery on the album. The next page appeared initially to be just another playbill. It was folded from the bottom, though, and all that was visible, in addition to 'Three nights only, no late entries' was, in letters going all the way across the page, 'BEANO'.

Vickers carefully unfolded the poster, which was for a show in Brighton in the summer of 1913, to reveal an illustration of Beano riding a unicycle and juggling either poorly illustrated hedgehogs or quite accurately depicted boot brushes.

'Also featuring...' appeared beneath Beano, with an illustration of two trapeze artists. Each had been captured the moment he released his trapeze and, as they flew through the air, they juggled brass rings between them.

Vickers neatly reanimated my drink. "Has this some bearing on the mystery, sir?"

"Well, for one thing, it seems to imply that at one point it was Beano the younger brother who was the bigger draw," I explained. "But of even greater interest is the legend beneath the lesser acrobats: 'Also featuring… Malandrino the Magnificent and the Daring Digby.'"

Vickers and I shared a glance of spoiled abundance, if that's something that can be distilled into a glance.

"Do you get the impression, Vickers, as I do, that if you keep turning the pages of that thing you'll eventually make a strong case that you and I killed Malandrino the Magnificent?"

"There does appear to be little to recommend any one line of enquiry over another," sympathised Vickers.

"Indeed. We've got the full cast list — scorned biddies, heart-broken commodores, disingenuous Boisjoly matriarchs, jealous brothers, malicious circus moguls… do you know what we need, Vickers?"

"Yes, sir." Vickers replaced my glass with the very latest thing in scotch and soda.

"Correct," I commended. "Now all we need is a sign of some sort."

And there was a knock at the door.

"Hullo." I watched Vickers weave over and open the door.

"Good afternoon, madam," he said. "It's most gratifying to see you again."

"Hello Vickers," said Mama or someone who sounded exactly like her. "Is Mister Boisjoly at home to visitors?"

Vickers stepped back and announced "Mrs Boisjoly, sir."

"What ho, Pinocchio," I hailed. "I was going to pop round yours, as it happens, for a spot of truth, but then I remembered that you never keep any on hand."

"Don't be tiresome, Anty, we have something important to discuss." Mama marched to the divan and installed herself on it like a flagpole on an uncharted island. "Whisky and water, please, Vickers."

Vickers depleted the precious stores and fluttered a glass of rare reserve onto a marble occasional at Mama's elbow. "Will that be all, sir?"

Vickers made good his escape and Mama steadied herself with what appeared to be a much-needed whisky. She's not easily shaken, Mama, so I prepared myself for a reckoning of consequence.

"It's your Aunt Jacqueline and her daughter, Chadwick," announced Mama. "They're stealing from the casino."

CHAPTER ELEVEN

Rigging Roulette
at the Riviera Royale

"No one can steal from a casino," I contended.

"Jacqueline and Chadwick have found a way," insisted Mama. "I've seen it myself, and so have the biddies."

"Very well, Mumford, what makes you think Aunt Jacqueline and Chadwick are cheating the casino?"

"I didn't, initially, I confess." Mama swirled her drink and then tasted it again with more consumer discretion. "Glen Glennegie?"

"Pre-war," I confirmed. "Toppers?"

"Please." I retrieved the decanter while Mama continued, "This afternoon the biddies made to me the most extraordinary proposition — they offered me half a million francs."

"That's about four thousand pounds," I guessed. "You're quite sure it's not the biddies leading a life of crime? What did they want for their money? An ounce of honesty? A half an ounce? I know you sell it dearly."

"They weren't just offering me four thousand pounds, Anty," said Mama coolly. "They were offering me four thousand *more* pounds."

"More than what?"

"More than they had already invested with Jacqueline and Chadwick. They're a gambling syndicate, and they thought I was in on it."

"Are you?"

"Anty, please, this is very grave."

"There's nothing wrong with forming a gambling syndicate, Mama," I pointed out. "Well, nothing illegal, let us say. It's invariably a mistake to pool your stake with friends. Takes almost all the fun out of losing your shirt."

"They're not losing, Anty," said Mama severely. "They're winning. Rather a lot."

"So? So do you."

"No, I don't. I often have good fortune and for some reason when I'm bank at baccarat opposing players tend to make poor decisions, but I'm not cheating."

"What makes you think Jacqueline and Chadwick are?"

"It's very subtle." Mama looked into her whisky for the sympathy I was failing to deliver. "Doubtless you won't believe me."

"Faddle and fleard, Mama," I proclaimed. "What reason have you ever given me to disbelieve you?"

"They almost never lose, Anty," explained Mama.

"More faddle and fathoms of fleard," I differed. "I was with Chadwick only this afternoon when she drew *vingt-trois* at *vingt-et-un*. That's *deux* too many."

"And then what did she do?"

"Quit. She's a sensible girl. And we had an appointment with Thumpy."

"That's all? She didn't signal the croupier, or trade places with her mother?"

"She certainly spoke with the dealer," I admitted. "She knew him from his days as a connoisseur of the second-round concussion. And she did perform an odd ritual with a monocle. That doesn't prove anything, though — clubmate of mine, Lobes Lillibins, had a very strict gambling routine, too — every time he ended a Saturday of long odds at Hurst Park out of pocket he'd break his umbrella over his knee. Had to order them in by the dozen."

I noticed, as I spoke and paced the room, that the mahogany

case was in full view. I positioned myself before it and, as a pretext, released the wasp from the sugar bowl. It shot out of captivity like a bullet from a gun on what should have been a direct course for the wide open balcony doors but, drunk with refined sugar, it instead knocked itself silly on a metal etching of Queen Victoria, seen discovering the planet Neptune above the credenza. This amused Mama only briefly, and she returned to her wild tales.

"Anty, I hardly credit it myself, but obviously the cards are marked in some fashion invisible to the naked eye, but detectable by special lens."

"And Chadwick is employing this miracle technology to determine when to walk away from the table," I surmised.

"Exactly."

"And the dealer is complicit."

"Obviously."

"And they've identified an imperfection in the roulette wheel that allows them to predict with some accuracy whether the ball will fall on black or red, determined by the spin of a coin on the betting area."

"Of… I… suppose something like that." Mama lowered a suspicious eye on me. "Certainly I've watched them play roulette for an entire evening and guess correctly almost every time. It must be some sort of trick."

"Yes, I saw them in action," I recalled. "I assumed it was a fluke. You say they can reproduce this phenomenon?"

"Practically without fail." Mama returned her glass to the occasional so that she could focus her energies on a single stern glare. "Anty, you have to stop them, before Rémy discovers what they're doing."

"Stop them?" I asked. "How can I stop them?"

"You must speak to them, Anty," said Mama with the tone of one describing the stark obvious to a simpleton. "Explain to them that the scandal would be ruinous. We'd never be able to show our faces again on the Riviera."

This prospect was enough to freeze the marrow. Firstly, it wasn't much of an exaggeration. If it's anything casinos like, it's taking money off punters and if there's anything they like even more it's keeping it. The trace of a hint that someone has worked out a scheme for tilting the playing field towards the player or merely horizontal is all the grounds every house from Marseille to Menton would need to feature the suspect on the front page of Chuckers-Out Gazette. Furthermore, Jacqueline and Chadwick would be banned, of course, but so would everyone they know and marry, and the Riviera is a second London to the migratory British Boisjoly. We come for the sun, of course, and the gentle seas and stunning views and sport racing and embarrassing luxury, but above all we come to rue mathematics at the roulette table. To be barred from the casinos of the *Cote d'Azur,* for a Boisjoly, would be like being barred from the bars of London, for a Boisjoly.

"Wouldn't they just deny it?" I asked.

"Of course, Anty," scolded Mama. "Obviously you'll have to work out how they're doing it. They can hardly feign innocence in the face of a scientific deconstruction of their methods."

"A scientific deconstruction of their methods, you say." I sipped a smug of whisky. "And what makes you think me capable of a deconstruction of methods, scientific or otherwise?"

Mama raised her eyebrows and lowered her chin, as though regarding me over imaginary pince-nez. "Didn't you say that you had discovered an unforeseen talent for defraying awkward situations?"

"Not so very unforeseen as all that, I don't think. You'll recall it was at the precocious age of seven that I contrived to convince you that the house was being fumigated for two days so that Etheline, the first downstairs maid, and Meriman, the second footman, could use our garden for their wedding reception."

"I recall nothing of the sort."

"Oh, right, no you wouldn't, would you," I realised. "Setting that aside indefinitely, of course I'll work out how — and if — Aunt Jacqueline and Chadwick are cheating the casino. Would you mind, in return, doing me a small service?"

"What nature of service?" asked Mama with profound

disinterest, as though enquiring on what day my birthday fell.

"Show me the mahogany box, the one from Aspinall's, in which came the diamond necklace Papa presented you on the occasion of your tenth anniversary."

"Why?"

"To bring me pleasure," I claimed. "I wish to reminisce of the occasion."

"You were eight."

"I'm flattered you recall. May I see the box?"

"I didn't bring it with me to Cap Royale."

"Yes, you did. It's not in your room in Kensington."

"How do you come to know that?"

"I searched your room," I said. "I had need of a hat pin, for the purposes of an important diplomatic gesture towards the chairman of the Juniper events committee."

"And you noticed and recalled the absence of a mahogany jewellery case."

"I have an eye for these things."

"And now you have a sudden impulse to see it."

"Very sudden, yes. Very impulsive."

"And this is nothing to do with the fact that the box in question is, at this very moment, on the table behind you?"

"Well?"

"Well, what?"

"Well, where do you think I found it?" I asked although, I contend, I shouldn't have needed to.

"In Malandrino's steamer trunk, no doubt," Mama drew cooly and calmly on her whisky. "I looked everywhere else."

Mama's stony countenance betrayed no emotion, but it appeared by some subtle air to be working harder than usual to do so. Perhaps her eye reflected some spot of errant light, or a slightly stertorous breath was drawn.

"Do you want to tell me how your necklace came to be in the possession of Malandrino the Magnificent?" I asked, as gently as something like that can be asked.

"No, Anty, I do not." Mama drew on her drink and focused on a point in the middle distance. "I gave it to him. On the night of the launch party I took it back."

"I think I need to know why you gave a necklace worth 20,000 pounds to a clown."

"He could be very charming, Anty." Mama finally looked me in the eye. "Very flattering."

"Then why did you take it back?"

"I recognised how foolish I was being," she said, as though talking about someone else who hadn't really been all that terribly foolish. "I saw Malandrino speaking to the biddies. Taking each of them to the side, during Beano's show, and whispering in their ears. I realised that I was just like them, or would soon be."

"Is that all that happened between you two that night? You took back your necklace?"

"Are you asking me if I murdered Malandrino?"

"It's a broad question, Mama, that seeks only to elicit detail," I explained. "Did you see anything, for instance, or did Malandrino say anything, or did you somehow leave him for dead in Thumpy's cage. It's this sort of minutia that matters in an investigation of this nature."

"I really was feeling seasick," said Mama with poise. "I used it as a pretext to go to Malandrino's stateroom. Then I asked him to let me wear the necklace at the party, and promised to return it to him later, before I left. Then I told him that I wished to be alone. When he left, I waited a few moments, then I left too."

"Neatly avoiding a scene," I observed. "He never asked for it back?"

"I never saw Malandrino again," said the most reflexive liar I've ever known. "That's the truth."

I remained unconvinced by much of what Mama had told me and by all that the biddies had told her. Cheating a casino, forsooth. Why would Aunt Jacqueline need to steal from anyone? And Chadwick? Would a perfect angel even understand the concept? Well of course not. Perfect angels, when confronted with the very idea of deception, probably just cock their heads and look at it with a sort of comely confusion.

So at the risk of adding yet another reckoning to the overdue queue, I went biddy-hunting, and I found a Digby.

In fact, I rambled the long way round the point in an evasive manoeuvre designed to avoid confronting Aunt Jacqueline without a full command of the facts, and was distracted by something shiny. The port had taken on something of the air of a mediaeval carnival with banners, streamers, horns, fire-breathers, funambulists, contortionists and clowns. There were perhaps a dozen gangly tumblers in a spirited frenzy of arms and legs and colleagues throwing one another into the air at seemingly very short notice. This chaotic coil raised the dust of the square under the baffled gaze of four grizzled salts, trying to exhaust the island's supply of Pernod and settle the Stalin question, and Deebee Digby.

"What ho, Diggers." I joined him dockside where he stood waving his arms about, directing the maelstrom like a deaf orchestra conductor, but otherwise resembling a lion-tamer in safari suit and patent-leather riding boots.

"Hullo, Anty." Digby glanced away only long enough to establish my identity. "You're not a contortionist by any chance, are you?"

"I literally have a man who ties my shoes for me, Deebee. Why? Are you short one?"

"I am...op, no, there she is, in that violin case." Deebee raised his voice, then, to call out to a wedge-shaped man with legs like an airedale and shoulders like a Clydesdale, "Stromboli, don't bend all the cannonballs now, we need them for Saturday. Practice on some coconuts or something." He shook his head with paternal forbearance. "Honestly, Anty, they're just like children."

"You're not tempted to show them how it's done, Deebee?"

"You ever try to bend a cannonball, Anty?"

"I was being coy, in that captivating way I'm told I have," I confessed. "Did you know that Malandrino's steamer trunk has been recovered?"

"Was it ever uncovered?"

"It had been thrown overboard."

"Oh, right, recovered — why was it thrown overboard?"

"Presumably to eliminate something that was in it."

"Why not just throw the thing overboard?"

"Obviously, Deebee, because the item in question was in the trunk and the trunk was locked."

"Makes simple sense, now you say it."

"It's a matter of perspective," I explained. "Can I ask why you neglected to mention that you and Malandrino had an act together?"

"Did I?" asked Deebee distractedly. "I thought I told you we started out together." He turned an earnest eye on mine. "Hang on… I did tell you. You were asking if Malandrino was taking his act solo, and I told you he'd never do that to me. We were like brothers, Anty. Not like Malandrino and Beano — we were like the kinds of brothers who like each other."

"I concede the point," I said. "I for some reason assumed that you were always as I see you now. I still have a coy card to play, though — perhaps you'd care to explain why you claimed that you never left the bow of the yacht during the party."

"I never did."

"You implied most vividly that you were on the bow," I differed, "when you said that the commodore was not."

"Yes, very well, I went looking for the commodore." Deebee effected to focus on the tumble and turmoil in the square.

"Did you find him?"

"No. I mean to say… no."

"Why not?"

"Because I wasn't really looking for him." Deebee turned a frank and vaguely sympathetic squint on me. "I was following Malandrino and… well…"

"And my mother."

"You know."

"I do."

"Oh, well. I guess that's all right then." Deebee brightened in a deliberate, provisional sort of way, as though trying cheerful on for size. "Is it?"

"She's a grown woman. And a widow."

"Still might have been awkward. It's why I didn't tell you I'd left the bow. And it's why I had to hide in a lifeboat so they wouldn't know I saw them."

"Did you see anyone else?" I asked.

"No. I heard someone leave the stateroom and walk past me towards the back of the boat. I kept my head down for a bit and it's a good thing I did, because I heard someone else follow a few minutes later."

"But you don't know who."

"Afraid not." Deebee looked back to the square and called, "Gretel — cease immediately juggling that violin case. It's fragile."

"What's all this in aid of, Deebs?" I asked. "I understood from Commodore Wairing that the troupe was joining the cruise at Saint Tropez."

"Had to change all that, didn't I? The first show is going to be right here, on the beach. I cabled the cast to get these printed." Deebee withdrew a folded pink handbill from his inside pocket. "They've been putting on teaser shows in every town square between here and Saint Tropez, handing these out by the fistful." He handed me the paper. "It's going to be huge, Anty."

I unfolded the handbill:

> 'This Saturday, one show only and ever...
>
> Delight at Europe's cleverest clowns...
>
> Marvel at the world's most audacious acrobats...
>
> Thrill to trapeze artists as they fly over shark-infested whirlpools...
>
> And then, witness for the first time in history...
>
> The dramatic and spectacular execution by electrocution of a killer elephant'

CHAPTER TWELVE

Anty's Aunty Raises the Ante

"It's not stealing, Mister Boisjoly…" claimed Mimpley.

"…it's only cheating," completed Biddicomb.

"You do yourselves a disservice, ladies," I countered. "It's both."

We were on the cocktail terrace, enjoying our 'fin gimlets' (two parts gin, one part anchovy paste) and watching Deebee organise a flotilla of skiffs to Little Miss Fortune. The sun had dropped behind the dome of the casino and lit it up like a biblical omen.

The biddies were dressed for an evening of aggressive bystanding. Biddicomb, in an orange, sausage-casing tube dress and birds' nest fascinator tangled in her hair, complete with taxidermied Goldcrest, exhibited the keen, fervent figure of a dark horse entry in a cutthroat evening of competitive knitting. Mimpley was in black and white classic choirmaster, hair ratcheted back, ready at an instant's notice to assume command of a book club.

"But, we're not doing either…" maintained Mimpley.

"…Jacqueline and Chadwick are doing the actual cheating," blamed Biddicomb.

"And, you thought, my mother," I noted.

"She does so very well at baccarat…"

"...we just assumed that she was in on it."

"There's very little skill and strategy to baccarat," I said, "but it's unique among casino games in that it's played between punters. The position of bank, which my mother typically occupies with the same subtle diplomacy with which Napoleon occupied Lisbon, affords the only slight advantage. What you saw as cheating was merely that advantage plus Mama's stern gaze, which I've seen cause grown men to pour tea into the biscuit bowl. You can imagine the effect on someone struggling with the portentous question of drawing or standing on five."

"Oh," regretted the biddies.

"Oh, indeed," I agreed. "Her bridge club makes her wear smoked glasses. But you say that Jacqueline and Chadwick are cheating for real, and with your money."

"Oh, yes, Mister Boisjoly..."

"...and doing very well."

"So my spies tell me," I said.

"You should watch them from the mezzanine..."

"...like we do. Every evening."

"Any idea how they're doing it?" I asked.

The biddies looked at each other. I detected a rare whatsit of dissent between them.

"Hypnosis." Mimpley spoke with the cool confidence of one who believes herself to be 'in the know'. "They dazzle the croupiers. I've seen them do it with a coin at the roulette wheel — one of them spins a shiny coin and the other sort of... moves about... giving instructions."

"Of course it's not hypnosis." Biddicomb said 'hypnosis' as though it was synonymous with 'alchemy'. "They're obviously using magnets. The coin has enough force to influence the roulette wheel."

"That's very nice, Myrtle," said Mimpley, as though to a simple child. "And do magnets change the cards dealt at *vingt-et-un?*"

"No, not magnets," conceded Biddicomb. "But something a good deal more scientific than hypnosis."

"She uses a special monocle," Mimpley confided to me, "to look into the dealer's subconscious."

"It's fair to say, then, ladies, that we're somewhere shy of a consensus on the point," I said. "Perhaps you could shed some light on another matter, then — what did Malandrino say to you that night on the boat?"

"Why, nothing, Mister Boisjoly." Mimpley stuck to her story.

"We didn't speak to him," stuck Biddicomb too.

"The truth, ladies, is like an anchovy cocktail — sometimes distasteful, often grey and smelly, and you haven't touched yours yet. I know that you each spoke to Malandrino that night."

The biddies shared another unspoken message, this time much more harmonious. Sad and resigned, but harmoniously so.

"He broke it off…" said Mimpley, quietly to her fin gimlet.

"…said this is it…" whispered Biddicomb to her hands.

"…the final…"

"…farewell."

"And then he went off…"

"…with Mrs Boisjoly."

"Implying what, if I may ask," I asked anyway.

"Oh, nothing at all, Mister Boisjoly…"

"…at least, not now."

"Yes, not now. It's why we thought your mother would understand…"

"…and want to help us."

"She's one of us, now."

"One of us."

"And what would you say are the chief obligations of membership?" I enquired.

"To love Malandrino…"

"…and to loathe him."

"And to have been played for a fool by him," I suggested.

"Yes." Mimpley said this to Biddicomb, who passed it to me seasoned with a tone of quiet regret, "We gave him ever so much money."

"We imagine your mother did, too."

"No comment," I commented. "Is this what's turned you to a life of crime, then? Or has the club been sticking up banks and robbing racetracks as a rite of initiation since inception?"

Once again the biddies bantered a sort of morse code composed of eyebrow flicker and pout, and then Biddicomb translated for my benefit, "We only really realised a... what would you call it?"

"A common purpose," suggested Mimpley.

"Yes, a common purpose. We only discovered a common purpose after Malandrino died."

"We've been rivals for so long and then, suddenly, we only had each other."

"And the circus."

"Yes, and the circus."

"It's all we know."

"It's all we've known."

"For... oh dear..."

"...ten years."

"Short pit stop, if we might, ladies, to take in the scenery and allow Anty to catch up," I proposed. "What has swindling a casino to do with life under the big top?"

"You see, we pooled our little all..." clarified Biddicomb.

"...but it wasn't enough," muddied Mimpley.

"Enough for what?" I asked. "You offered my mother what she described as 'another' four thousand pounds. How much is the betting syndicate worth at this point?"

"Eight thousand pounds," answered Mimpley.

"Twelve thousand, had your mother been game," answered Biddicomb. "Not counting what Jacqueline and Chadwick have won."

"And that's not enough? Are you planning to start your own circus?"

"No, of course not," scoffed Biddicomb.

"We're going to buy the *Cirque d'Azur.*"

I took up my gimlet which had, for the duration, been neglected and lonely, and employed it as a distraction while I took a good, anthropological gawk at the biddies. They presented very convincingly as camp-followers. As spurned infatuates they might have been training for the role from childhood. Even as conspirators to defraud a casino they had a certain fatalistic, ironic adaptability to purpose, the way a fountain pen makes a perfectly serviceable corkscrew when you find yourself without one after rowing all the way to the middle of the Serpentine. But circus moguls, I had come to believe, to a man were defined by a certain cold-blooded Digbyness that the biddies lacked in buckets. I didn't see it.

"I don't see it," I said.

"Well, you will…" assured Biddicomb.

"...just as soon as Jacqueline and Chadwick wind things up," reinforced Mimpley.

"You don't mean to continue down this treacherous road to shame and exile."

"How can we not, Mister Boisjoly?" asked Mimpley.

"I think the train, as they say, has left the station," Biddicomb elucidated with a helpful transportation metaphor. "It's not as though we can just give the money back to the casino."

❦

I accompanied the biddies inside to where the terrace becomes a mezzanine overlooking the casino floor. They installed themselves at their bistro table observatory and I leaned over the ornate iron railing, sipping my gimlet and projecting such cool indifference I might have been woven into the background of one of the tapestries of Vicky discovering the atom or planning the London Underground. Thusly installed, I cast a casual eye over the players at the roulette table.

It was a choice moment. In a blur of activity, Chadwick reached past her mother to snatch up her spinning coin, the pearl landed on thirty-five black, the commodore, who was sitting across from the ladies, dropped his head to his hands and mother and daughter performed a little ritual two-step. Jacqueline gathered up two enormous stacks of winnings and handed them to her daughter, who stalked straight-legged towards the *vingt-et-un* table. Jacqueline watched her approvingly, then looked up and straight into my eyes. She issued a knowing wink that seemed, in the moment, audible, and then made for the stairs.

"Hello, Anty," she said, as she swept onto the mezzanine and continued towards the stained-glass doors. "See if you can't find a waiter on your way, there's a good lad." And I followed.

Evening had become night in that sudden way of coastal basins enclosed by cliffs. The moon was a slim and simple-minded smile, flashing a guileless grin and then hiding behind furtive nighttime clouds. Beyond the terrace the sea was already black and Little Miss Fortune was only represented by running lamps at bow and stern. But the terrace glowed with the interior light filtered through the maritime greens of the stained-glass wall, and the air was warm and still and perfumed as though for a long-ish evening at the opera.

Jacqueline sashayed across the terrace and did a *fouetté* (from third position) into a chair at a table overlooking the port. She flicked back her mainsail and slipped a cigarillo between her lips and snapped her fingers. At least, I think she snapped her fingers. It may have been more of an impression. She might have just batted her eyelashes. In any case, something snapped. Rémy, who may well have been minding the reception desk at the time, rushed onto the scene and lit Jacqueline's little cigar. She had ordered a bottle of champagne and Rémy had scampered off to provide it before I even made it to the table.

"Anty, darling, I've been so looking forward to having you all to myself. I hear such lovely things about your money."

"What ho, long lost legacy." I reflexively took my spot across from her, as though the scene had been blocked out in advance by a fussbudget theatre director. This reckoning had started weakly out of the gate and I felt I'd already somehow ceded the upper hand. "Another lucky evening at the wheel, I see."

Jacqueline drew heavily on her cigarillo and launched a succession of smoke rings into the night air. "You know perfectly well that luck doesn't enter into it, Anty."

"Do I?" I asked innocently. "I'm not sure that I do. I've managed to maintain quite a consistent streak without resorting to cheating. Royal Ascot before last, I blindly chose the last horse in every single race, with the exception of the Gold Cup, for which my selection was scratched. I came to be known as the Pick of Death. Even chaps I didn't know were asking me who I liked least in each fixture, and putting their shirts on it."

Rémy materialised out of the darkness with a champagne pop and finessed two *coupes* onto the table between us. We waited discreetly while he fizzed up our glasses and fizzled away.

"Gambling is for those who have nothing better on which to spend their luck," pronounced Jacqueline. "The risk of getting caught is far, far more invigorating than the risk of losing. Besides, I don't like losing. Tried it once. Didn't care for it at all."

"One habituates," I reassured her from the lofty ledge of experience. "So you admit to cheating."

"I admit only to winning against all probability, Anty." Jacqueline regarded me through a cloud of her own making. "Winning is only cheating if you care about the rules."

This was, to me, novel. Up until that very moment I'd have instinctively and instantly classified those who flout the house rules among those hungry-looking fellows with stringy beards at Hyde Park Corner who counsel the evisceration of the clubbing classes as somehow essential to the seizure of the means of production. But here was the mother of the woman I loved, herself a fetching and fascinating variant of the species, advocating for the downfall of society.

"But… they're the house rules," I pointed out. "And cheating can get you barred."

"Winning can get you barred," countered Jacqueline.

"From an individual casino, certainly, but rarely from an entire coastline, and that's what's at stake."

"Chaddy told me that you were a sportsman." Jacqueline fired a shot of smoke across my bow.

"And so I am," I insisted. "Famous for it. It's widely understood by the better bits of London society that if there's one way to get Anty Boisjoly to try to outrun a policeman across Westminster Bridge it's to bet him that he can't. For the record, he can't, but it's not for lack of sporting blood. As is so often the case with these things, it came down to the psychological aspect, and the bobby in question was given to believe that I had pinched his helmet."

"How did he get that idea?"

"I was wearing it," I said. "That slowed me considerably as well. Throws off your balance. If you ever try it, remember to budget for the extra weight up top."

"Very diverting, Anty." Jacqueline smiled indulgently through the cloud. "Have you ever been thrown out of Maxim's?"

"Of course."

"Because you danced with Coco Chanel's escort?"

"Candidly, I don't recall the details," I said. "It can't be entirely discounted."

"Ever bluff your way onto Douglas Fairbanks' yacht?"

"Have you?"

"I never need to bluff, Anty." Jacqueline took a victory sip of champagne and expelled another stream of smoke over the terrace railing. "Reggie Vanderbilt once offered me a yacht if I'd help him establish grounds for divorce."

"Did you?"

"Of course I didn't, Anty," said Jacqueline, scandalised.

"Have you any idea how much trouble a yacht is?"

"Not much of a boat person, in fact," I admitted. "I have had tea on board the royal yacht, though. There's no record of it, unfortunately — the Queen Mum somehow took me for the Grand Vizier Pasha, in the incognito tuxedo from Constantinople for a high-level natter, and I didn't know the protocol for setting straight a dowager queen. I probably should have come through with something, though, because just as we were wading into the cucumber sandwiches the real thing apparently requested permission to board and wound up below decks for the remainder of the afternoon with chaps who know a thing or two about hot lights and pointed questions. Turkish troops crossed the Dardanelles the next morning."

"I recall," Jacqueline said with a sort of dreamy recollection. "I was in Dinard that summer, when Picasso painted *Buste de femme les bras levés.*"

"Oh, right. That's quite famous. I've seen it."

"I'm in it."

"Of course you are."

"Pablo can be such a darling." Jacqueline created a cloud into which she looked at memories. "He called me his muse."

"Not really."

"He used that word rather a lot," admitted Jacqueline. "He often called the girl who delivered the bread his muse. And a stray cat, briefly, until it stole an entire camembert off the window sill."

"It's just, I thought, Picasso has a rather conspicuous preference for the apple-cheeked, milk-maid type, while you're, much more…"

"Old?"

"I was going to say refined."

"What the dear devil is wrong with wrinkles?" wondered Jacqueline aloud. "I'd rather look good for my age than haggard for my youth."

"You have a very charming daughter." That, for the record, was the point at which I realised that I had entirely lost control of the narrative. My reckoning had transformed into a suitability interview.

"And she's only going to get better. She tells me that you, at least, are well situated."

"I typically have something left over at the end of the month," I said with the cool, detached angst of a gentleman discussing money.

"I don't need to hear it." Jacqueline wafted the question away on an ephemeral grey plume. "My daughter knows that it never matters how much money a man says he has, so long as he can prove it. The main thing is never be dull. You're not dull, are you Anty?"

"Would that I were," I said. "You know I don't believe I've seen a Sunday morning since my christening. Often of a hazy, headachy afternoon at Bow Street Nick I find myself wishing I could learn more retiring habits."

"One cannot be taught to be dull, it's a skill acquired through tireless hesitation. Have you ever jumped out of an aeroplane?"

"This again," I lamented. "No, I have never jumped out of an aeroplane, and as this appears to be such a deep line in the sand for so many people you may as well know that I never will. I've never even been on an aeroplane and if, in the vanishingly thin likelihood I ever am, it will be with a firm guarantee that everyone can and will remain on board until the aircraft has come to a complete halt."

"Ever skied down a sheer slope?"

"Deliberately?"

"Yes."

"Then I'll have to say no."

"Ever taken an Alfa Romeo all out?"

"That depends almost entirely on what you're talking about," I replied. "Is that one of those American cocktails with altogether too much fruit juice?"

"It's a racing car."

"And by 'all out' you mean to say..."

"Top speed. About a hundred and twenty miles per hour."

"I believe I misheard."

"It's exhilarating," claimed Jacqueline. "You must try it."

"I will," I assured her. "Immediately after I jump out of an aeroplane, after which I may do a little light bullfighting. I take it you've done so?"

"No, but I was in Pamplona with Hemingway when he fell into the *Plaza de Toros* while trying to retrieve a bottle of *Fundador,*" reminisced Jacqueline. "Turned out to be empty, but I suspect that he would have found another reason to fall into the *Plaza de Toros.*"

"Doubtless," I agreed. "But I was referring to the aforementioned Alfalfa Martini."

"Oh, that. No." Jacqueline breathed dreamy mists from her nostrils. "Bugatti. I drove the winning car in the Monte Carlo Grand Prix."

"You did, did you?" I hadn't actually suspected until then that Aunt Jacqueline's stories might have been just so much spun sparkle, and I wasn't entirely certain what I ought to do with this bald claim. "I thought that was a chap named Grover-Williams." Well, apparently I did know what to do with it.

Jacqueline laughed indulgently. "I don't mean I won the race — I drove the winning car once through the city. Louis insisted — I had a small hand in getting the Monaco Grand Prix recognised by the French Automobile Association."

"That would be Prince Louis II," I clarified. "The notorious baccarat bandit."

"You know him?"

"I'm among his greatest supporters," I said. "Not entirely willingly, but you can't choose your cards. At least, I can't. Would you care to tell me how you manage it?"

"Half the fun, Anty, is the challenge of getting away with it."

"I understand entirely," I said. "And now you've been caught, that challenge is at an end. Mama will be pleased to hear it."

"You only know that I'm doing it, Anty dear." Jacqueline tapped a gold lacquered fingernail on her empty coupe. "You haven't caught me until you've figured out how I do it. You said you were a sportsman."

"Down to my last collar stud." I topped up our champagne glasses.

"Then let's make it interesting." Jacqueline raised her glass in a Faustian toast. "You work out how I'm doing it, and I'll stop. You don't, and you have to join the betting syndicate."

And in a stroke this Machiavellian marvel had raised the stakes beyond rescuing. I was playing for the Boisjoly right of residence on the Riviera, my reputation as a sportsman and the strength of my claim on Chadwick's hand. And I had no choice but to accept.

"Very well, I accept your terms," I said. "I ask only that whatever happens, you keep this particular skeleton in the back of the closet. If you can manage it, behind something heavy."

"Not really in my nature, Anty," confided Jacqueline. "I'm forced to keep all my skeletons on display — there's simply no room in my closet for anything that flamboyant."

CHAPTER THIRTEEN

The Flume and Form of the Looming Storm

I awoke, as was spasmodic custom on the Riviera, to an explosion.

"Rémy has malfunctioned," I said to Vickers, who was drawing the curtains and allowing an early, gloomy grey to ooze into the room. "It's still dark out."

"That was not the midday cannon, sir." Vickers assembled a platter of clatter on the vanity. "It was thunder. The weather is most inclement and, while it is early, the darkness is largely the effect of cloud cover."

"Ah, yes, it all comes back to me now — I left instructions for an early call," I recollected. "So, this is what mornings are like, are they?" I received the cup of calm. "I don't think I care for them at all."

"Tropical storms are infrequent but inevitable features of the coast, sir, and it's entirely coincidental that this one should occur in the morning."

Vickers proceeded to the wardrobe, which he opened and contemplated as though it was hanging in the National Gallery.

"Dress me for action, today, Vickers," I said. "I'm on a tight schedule. I need to absolve Thumpy of murder before execution day tomorrow, and still find time to observe the Quillfeather Gang in action this evening at the casino."

"Has Mrs Boisjoly formed a gang?"

"Mama? Probably. Be a good career path for her," I speculated. "But I'm referring to the perilous pastime that Aunt Jacqueline and Chadwick have invented for themselves — they're cheating the casino."

"I find that difficult to credit, sir."

"As would I, were there not witnesses," I said. "Including the aforementioned Mrs Boisjoly. And it gets worse — they've formed a betting syndicate."

"This is most alarming, sir." Vickers withdrew a navy serge double-breasted from the wardrobe and held it up to the light. "The consequences for Mrs Boisjoly and yourself, should this be discovered, would be very grave."

"Which is why Mama put me on the case." I cast a judgemental eye over the suit. "Too officious, Vickers. Let us have something bright, light, and slight. The better to move undetected among the natives."

"The serge is better suited to prevailing weather conditions, sir." Vickers held an admittedly dashing blue and white diagonally pencil-striped tie against the suit.

"The weather, in my bitter experience, Vickers, is constantly changing," I observed. "It is unreliable. Unlike, say, that banana-coloured linen blazer. Just the thing for when the sun comes back out, as it inevitably will. We must always plan for such contingencies."

"Very good, sir."

"It's chummier, too," I added. "A quality not to be underestimated as I contrive to tickle the truth out of a boatload of liars. Have you ever played Three-card Monte, Vickers?"

"In my younger days, sir." Vickers matched the banana-coloured blazer with a grape-coloured tie. "But my fingers are no longer sufficiently nimble."

"In fact I meant more in the role of victim," I said. "But, good to know. In any case, you know the general disposition of the pigeon — he focuses all his attention on a card, thinking it's the queen or, in this case, the jester, while all the other cards are off doing heaven-knows-what. Playing another game altogether, for all the mark knows."

"Fancifully put, sir, but in essence correct."

"Well, that's how I feel about the movements of everyone on board the yacht the night of the murder," I said. "As though I'm following the wrong card. For one thing, accountings have been fitful, at best, with most witnesses claiming they didn't want to sully my mother's good name."

"Most civil of them."

"They're probably just terrified of her."

"Quite possibly, sir."

"Nevertheless," I persevered, "we appear to have a matrix of reports that positions the playing board thusly — the biddies, Jacqueline and Chadwick were on the bow while, first, the commodore wanders off into the darkness. Then, feeling seasick, my mother is accompanied to his stateroom by Malandrino. Deebee follows. Minefield seizes the opportunity to extort the Beano, who storms off. Minefield follows. He loses him, however, and for some reason doesn't immediately return. Meanwhile Deebee, who has apparently hidden in a lifeboat, hears two people leave Malandrino's stateroom, separately, and ostensibly these same two people walk past his hideout in the direction of the stern."

"Most succinct recounting of the state of play, sir."

"Thank you. It helps that not a soul seems particularly interested in my investigations," I noted. "Even the biddies, who are balancing the loss of their mutual aspiration with a new-found common purpose, to wit; raising enough money to get into the circus game. The commodore is languishing in the world's longest and deepest run of bad luck, while Jacqueline and Chadwick are contriving to do the precise opposite. Max Minefield remains preoccupied with his ambition to bring to the world his bleak fable, set to music. The Beano is indifferent to the death of his brother, apart from noting that it makes him the headline act. Deebee, of course, is gleefully planning the pointless and painful demise of the world's most ingratiating elephant."

"And Mrs Boisjoly?" asked Vickers, only partially distracted by the delicate sock question.

"You know, Mama's the only one who seems to actually

miss Malandrino," I only just then realised. "It's most unnerving. Like discovering she's secretly saved a lock of my hair. In any case, where were we?"

"On the bow of the yacht, just prior to the fireworks demonstration."

"Exactly," I agreed. "Which started some ten minutes late. From this point on, no one will admit to having seen Malandrino alive again. The light show lasts half an hour to forty-five minutes, and then everyone but the commodore and Beano return to the island. On arrival at the dock, as you so capably determined, they were met by hotel staff and chaperoned to their rooms. Alibis all round."

I overruled Vickers yet again, this time in favour of light espadrilles instead of gum-soled oxfords, and then stepped onto the balcony to inure myself to the hour. It was, as expected, unnatural. There was no one thing wrong, as such, but the atmosphere was composed of differing, incompatible beats, like a perfectly competent horn section accompanying a whistling tea kettle.

I scanned the grey horizon from the west to the east where my attention lingered. There was something concrete, now, something clearly wrong with this bleary, blurry, soupy scene — Little Miss Fortune was gone.

The sea was lapis and lively, purple clouds moved slowly overhead and a brisk, briny breeze blew across the square before the hotel. I found myself rethinking my banana-coloured blazer — there was a buccaneering energy in the air that called for knee breeches and an eye-patch and a scabbard strapped to my hip with a broad leather belt the size of a cummerbund. I walked to the prow of the island and stood by the cannon and breathed in this invigorating mix of maritime morning.

"Helloooo, Mister Boisjoly."

A chorus of giddy, biddy energy called to me from the swimming cove below. I didn't see the ladies, initially, only their little rowboat, but then they waved and I realised that the bobbing buoys next to the boat were, in fact, yellow and red bathing caps. I stepped down the path and called back.

"What ho, castaways. Do you know you're on the wrong side of the hull?"

The biddies laughed with the robust abandon of the strong swimmer.

"We're practising holding our breath..." said Mimpley, then she puffed out her cheeks and went under.

"...and hunting sunken treasure," explained Biddicomb before pinching her nose and submerging just as Mimpley resurfaced.

"Oh... pox." I had overlooked, not for the first time, the vexatious habit consequences so often have of attaching themselves to my actions. "I say, ladies..."

"A treasure!" Mimpley burst the surface like a naval mine. She and Biddicomb hitched their elbows over the sides of the boat and examined something precious that Mimpley placed on the bench between them.

"It's very pretty, Bidelia," said Biddicomb.

"But I think it's just a rock, Myrtle."

"It's a treasure of a sort..."

"...and so we need only keep looking."

On the other hand, I reflected, the biddies were well out of trouble while seeking sunken treasure, and there was something about their pure satisfaction with a shiny pebble that put me in mind of something. I wasn't yet sure what — I knew only that it was something somehow material to one or both of the mysteries that needed solving by nightfall, and so I elected to not rock the boat.

"Right, oh, ladies," I said. "Just a matter of perseverance, I expect."

I wished the biddies luck and continued along the path towards the marina, all the while keeping an eye out for Little Miss Fortune, but the harbour was empty except for a light and layered rising of morning mist. The fog drifted ashore and mingled with the bistro tables of the square, and it swirled about my feet and those of Max Minefield, who was holding a bakelite cigarette holder to the flame of a small ceramic chafing dish on which rested a pewter coffee pot. As English custom and cuisine was to the Riviera Royale, so was Italian café culture to the fisherman's square.

"Morning, Max," I said, taking the liberty of the chair across from him.

"Good morning, Anty." Max smiled somehow earnestly — not so much as though he was happy to see me, exactly, as he was pleased that I wasn't just about anyone else. "Coffee?"

Minefield poured a tiny cup of viscous ooze that appeared to have been sourced fresh and unfiltered from a well in Texas, and then focussed all his emotional and physical means on breathing life into a cigarette through a tiny aperture several feet away.

"Doubtless you've been anxious to pick up where we left off…" Minefield held up a 'just a moment' hand, which is just as well, because I had nothing to say. "Before you speak, you should know that I, too, have been thinking about our partnership."

"Oh, right, well," I said. "Capital. You first."

"The ceiling of my theatre will need to be two hundred feet high." Again, Minefield stopped me from adding that which had yet to occur to me. "And I won't have you interfering with the story. Or the dialogue. Or music. Certainly not casting. Above all, not the lyrics. The lyrics are sacrosanct."

"Right oh."

"I didn't think that would sit well with you, but just listen to this…" Minefield tapped his cigarette holder on his coffee cup like a metronome. Presently, he nodded along with this accompaniment. And then, extraordinarily, he sang this…

> *"Nothing can make*
> *me fly higher*
> *Than you and me*
> *on a high wire*
> *I thought I'd make it better yet*
> *And soar without a safety net*

You know I never
would have risked it
If I'd known I
could have missed it

This is the chorus — entirely a capella...

Trapezy peasey
I feel quite queasy
When I'm on the ground
Trapezy peasey
If you ever need me
I'll come swinging round"

I think it likely I was staring, and it's very possible that my mouth drooped open.

"Catchy, what?" claimed Minefield.

"I certainly hope not."

"Well, there you have it." Minefield examined his cold cigarette end. "It's just that sort of remark that will prevent us from forming a creative dialectic. People like you, Anty, don't know how much words can sting."

"Right oh. I'll endeavour to learn from this experience, as I heal from it."

"I hope that you do, Anty."

"You know, I think I feel better already. Must be this coffee pudding. By the by, have you seen a steam yacht, recently, about yay big..." I held out my hands to frame the spot where Little Miss Fortune had been anchored. "Last seen roughly there."

"The commodore and Deebee took it round to the other side of the island early this morning... ah!" Minefield celebrated a victory sip of smoke from his bakelite straw before adding, "They're setting up the generator and switches for the execution."

CHAPTER FOURTEEN

The Abominable Facts of All Animal Acts

A flotilla of skiffs from Little Miss Fortune drifted into view and twirled helplessly and aimlessly towards port, and Minefield made good his escape.

"All ashore, Commodore," I said to Wairing as he climbed unsteadily onto the dock. He had about him a canvas tarpaulin and an aura of damp defeat. "You're looking chipper, skipper."

"Am I?"

"You trick the truth from me with honeyed words," I admitted. "You do not. In point of fact you look more like something Pilque would cut out of a net, and be glad to be rid of."

The commodore shuffled to my table and squished onto a chair. His captain's blazer was a shrunken, sunken wreck, and his polka-dotted ascot was missing, presumed lost at sea. "Not far off the truth. I fell in the water. Is that coffee?"

"Allow me... Op. All gone. Sorry."

"Of course it is." Wairing warmed his hands over the flames of the chafing dish which his dripping sleeves promptly extinguished. He sighed an expression of existential woe and we watched the tumblers and jugglers and Beanos of the circus tumble and juggle out of the boats and into the square.

"I gather that, against all odds, you had an even earlier morning than I, Commodore."

Wairing nodded blankly, staring into the memory of recent trauma. "It's surprisingly cold on the water at that hour. We had to collect a shipment of coal from Nice, and then drop anchor on the other side of the island."

"Did you forget to let go?"

"No." The commodore shivered under his sail-cloth cape. "We had to lay cables from the yacht to the shore. Heavier than you'd expect."

"I'm not sure that I would have any expectations of cables at all," I realised in the moment. "They could float for all I know."

"Well, they don't. They sink like stones, in fact, pulling a chap right out of a boat if he's not careful. Or if he's just plainly and consistently unfortunate."

"Just as well," I said. "You won't be needing any cables."

"Oh, the cables are just fine. Completely waterproof." The commodore said this with a tone of bitter admiration. "All that remains is to connect the big, theatrical button on the beach."

"Where does one get a big theatrical button at short notice?" I wondered. "No matter, it will be of no value either, nor will what I'm sure is a comically oversized executioner's hood. Before tomorrow I shall reveal the identity of the real killer."

"You know who did it?"

"Very nearly."

"You know how it was done, though."

"Not quite. I'm still sifting the evidence."

"But you've worked out why Malandrino was killed."

"This is presenting the greatest obstacle," I admitted. "I'm spoiled for choice. Furthermore, drawing frank disclosure from the interested parties has been like extracting healthy teeth. Do you know if Pilque hadn't caught the steamer trunk in his net I might never have known about Malandrino and Deebee's double act?"

"What's this about Pilque's net?"

"Pilque is a fisherman, Commodore," I elucidated. "A net is an indispensable tool of the trade."

"Oh, rather, I mean to say…"

"Without which I never would have learned that once upon a time it was Beano who was the headline act."

"Was he?"

"There was a playbill in the trunk attesting to the fact."

"Oh, yes?"

"And of course I learned of the sad injustice visited upon you and Penelope Fairweather by Malandrino the Magnificent," I concluded. "Care to tell me about it, Commodore?"

The commodore pulled his stiff cloak closer and effected to be distracted by the unicyclists balancing on the edge of the dock. "Not a great deal to add, I don't think."

"Malandrino stole your fiancée," I prompted. "And then broke her heart."

"Did I not mention that?"

"You did not," I said. "You left out the most motivational motive for murder when you saw that the steamer trunk was missing."

"I say, that's right, I did, didn't I?" The commodore returned his attention to me. "Proves I didn't kill Malandrino if I didn't know the trunk was missing, doesn't it?"

"Does it?"

"Doesn't it?" The commodore assumed the baffled countenance of one counting on his fingers. "Surely the killer chucked the trunk overboard."

"I don't know if that follows, Commodore. Any number of people had cause to eliminate what the trunk contained — it may have been a chucking-overboard of opportunity."

"Oh, yes, I see what you mean."

"Did you happen to see anyone shifting any steamer trunks that night?" I asked. "It would be very helpful if you could recall such a thing."

"No… no, nothing like that." The commodore gazed vaguely in the direction of Monte Carlo or, had it still been there, Little Miss Fortune. "It was too dark to actually see anyone, if you take my meaning."

"Unless your meaning is that you saw something else then no, I don't," I said.

"That's just it — I saw someone, but I didn't see him, you see."

"If I may infer, you saw someone but couldn't make out who it was."

"Fiddling about with the equipment, on the port side."

"The opposite side to Malandrino's stateroom."

"That's right. But I know who it was."

"You recognised this person by a silhouette of cut granite?" I asked. "Was it my mother?"

"No."

"You knew it was the Beano from his curly globe of hair?"

"No, not Beano."

"You recognised Deebee by his voice? Malandrino by his mouse ears?"

The commodore leaned over the cold chafing dish and spoke in confidential tones. "He was lighting that infernal cigarette."

The commodore retired to his room and a warm bath and a moment later the barman relit the chafing dish and laid on a fresh pot. The sun was rising from just behind the flat horizon and backlighting an immense bean stalk of a silhouette that sprouted next to my table. The shadow tipped slowly towards me and then broke into its constituent parts — one part unicycle, one part Astounding Bounding Bean.

He leaned a unicycle taller than a Beano against the fig tree and spun into the vacant chair in a manner that made the act of sitting down a spectacle for all ages.

"Boisjoly."

"Bean."

"Is that coffee?"

"It's a surprisingly solid facsimile thereof." I sliced off two cups. "How are rehearsals coming along?"

"Pure chaos." Beano bit into his coffee like a man with no

fear. "Fortunately, a performance surface formed of rocks, damp equipment, the company of graceless incompetents, and Deebee Digby's twisted final act pose no challenges to the Astounding Bounding Bean."

"Yes, lucky break, that," I agreed. "I take it you're among that twee crowd of anaemic sentimentalists who don't regard ritual murder as good theatre?"

"Do you?"

"More of a musical-comedy man, personally," I said. "Slightly to the fanciful side of *Funny Face,* but more coldly unsentimental than, say, *No, No, Nanette*, if it's not splitting hairs. Your views, however, must have changed since you last juggled a badger."

"Hedgehog." Beano shook another cup of coffee out of the pot. "How do you know about that?"

"There's little that escapes my attention, my dear Beano," I said with what theatre people call a subtext of detective-inspectoriness. "I also know, for instance, that Malandrino was your brother."

"Everybody knows that."

"Really? You didn't mention it."

"No," parried Beano. "Because everybody already knows it."

"Right oh," I conceded. "Does everybody also know that there once was a day when Malandrino was Sancho Panza to your Don Quixote?"

"He was what to my what?" asked Beano, vaguely pettishly. "Do you ever speak plainly, Boisjoly?"

"Sorry," I said. "Curse of a classical education. I meant to say he was Horatio to your Hamlet."

The Beano levelled on me a blank regard that was still somehow rich with meaning.

"You were the headline act," I explained.

The Beano turned with a deliberate nonchalance on the rehearsal in the square. "Audiences are fickle."

"Nothing to do with the hedgehogs, then."

"The Astounding Bounding Bean does not need to torment animals for the entertainment of the public..." Beano bit a bitter bite of brew, "...even if that's what the public demands."

"You gave your brother the animal act," I surmised, "and along with it your place at the top of the playbill."

"He stole them from me. He convinced me that I looked foolish and cruel, juggling innocent hedgehogs."

"Not a reachingly unreasonable hypothesis, from the layman's perspective."

"No, it isn't," admitted Beano, still gazing out to sea and into the past. "He showed me a review; 'If it hadn't been for the cries of horror from the audience, I might have believed myself at a child's birthday party.' I released the hedgehogs, and focused on my bounding."

"Well, lucky break for the hedgehogs, at the very least."

"The following season, Malandrino introduced his hedgehog juggling act," continued Beano. "Of course he'd concocted one of his fables — the hedgehogs were of a rare jungle breed, he claimed, the spines of which were highly venomous."

"Now you mention it — how does one juggle a hedgehog?"

"Some take the trouble to clip the spines," explained Beano. "I used to simply varnish the tips with spirit gum."

"Not really."

"Oh, yes, it's quite effective."

"I'm sure it is," I agreed. "'But I mean that it's extraordinary that there are competing schools of thought in spined rodent juggling."

Beano shrugged. "Not really. You get the same sort of thing with stilt-serpents and high-wire donkeys."

"Yes, I expect you would."

"But not, obviously, with bears and elephants."

"No, I can see that." I nodded knowingly. "One niggling point, though — why not?"

"Because they can kill you." Beano spoke with the flat authority of the obvious. "Malandrino used tranquillisers for the bears, and of course he trained that wretched elephant with a regimen of applied antagonism. It's little wonder my brother should die by the recoil of his own barrage."

"So you think Thumpy capable of taking revenge, do you?"

"Who else might have done it?" Beano pushed his cup away and rose from the table. "I understood that everyone was accounted for."

"Mostly, they are," I confirmed. "Up until the end of the party, when only two possible suspects remain at large — Commodore Wairing and the Astounding Bounding Bean."

"Not even them." Beano shook his head casually and even more casually levitated onto his stilticycle. "The commodore and I were both on board the yacht all night."

"Ah, but how can you be sure?"

"We were matching each other, stoop for stoop of grog…" said Beano from the top of his unicycle, "…and story for bitter story featuring the Malignant Malandrino."

I decided to take this new obstacle to breakfast on the terrace, and I'm glad that I did, for there on her own, seated by the rail beneath a personal ray of sunshine from a seraph-sized break in the cloud-cover, was Chadwick Quillfeather.

"What ho, hearth and home." I staked my claim to the opposing chair. "Just tucking in?"

"What ho, Anty." Chaddy cast off a smile that a lesser woman would have sold at a tidy profit, and then returned her attention to the bill of fare. "Maybe. Have you tried the braked ham?"

"I have," I said. "It's pressed crab, but otherwise you'd think it was the brunch gammon at Claridge's. Good morning, Rémy," I added, for Rémy had materialised at our side. "Braked ham for the lady, and I believe I'll try the flood pudding and slushy peas."

"A most choice choice, Anty," Rémy assured me. He plucked up the menus and coyly hid behind one them to say to me, "You have the little bonnet, as we say in the English, no?"

"We most certainly do, Rémy," I agreed. "Practically non-stop."

"Couple of mimosas, too, Rémy," diverted Chadwick.

"We're having champagne for breakfast?" I asked as Rémy disappeared in a puff of enthusiasm.

"It's almost noon." Chaddy looked skyward at the camouflaged sun.

"I know it is," I acknowledged. "I woke up early. I have a complex and vexing mystery to solve today. Two, if you count Malandrino's murder."

"Yes, mother mentioned your little wager." Chadwick rolled her napkin in that playful manner which, I just then discovered, I find alluring beyond description. "It's not typically advised to wager against my mother — she has a knack."

"Cheating is not a knack," I gently differed.

"She has a knack for cheating," revised Chadwick. "Whatever the reason, it almost always leads to heartache or, taking the clinical case study of the biddies as a handy f'r'instance, heartbreak."

"Is this in some fashion related to the betting syndicate?"

With a swift sleight-of-hand, Chadwick converted the napkin she'd been abusing into a swan, and placed it on the table between us. "Not directly. She told them that Malandrino was playing them off against each other. They didn't buy it, at first, so mother, sensing a sure thing, proposed a bet."

"Which, if she won, would require the biddies to join the gambling syndicate," I surmised.

"One point, Anty Boisjoly," said Chaddy.

"How did she prove it?"

"She didn't have to. She guessed — correctly — that the biddies need only compare the letters they'd received over the years from Malandrino."

"I have an idea how that worked out."

Chaddy turned her swan inside out and it became a frog. "For the best, in the end — the ladies lose a louse and gain gambling gold."

"Do you think that's the way they saw it?"

"Still waters." Chaddy flattened out her frog, turning it back into a napkin. "Hard to tell with fanatics, sometimes."

"Are you quite certain that you, your mother, Miss Mimpley and Miss Biddicomb were alone on the bow of the yacht for the duration?" I asked. "Nobody — such as either or both of the biddies — left at any point?"

"I don't think so." Chaddy glanced over her shoulder at the mountains. "Mother might be able to say. I'm not sure I'd have noticed everything that was going on behind me — night was falling and I was standing at the prow, watching the mountains disappear. It's quite an impressive trick. Wish I could master it. Can you imagine how handy that would be?"

"I hope you understand that you'll be expected, as the wife of a member of the Juniper club, to give up your life of crime."

Chadwick raised her eyebrows in a manner that expressed mirth and menace in equal measure, but in the same instant Rémy appeared with tall, ornamented mango mimosas.

"Dinner will be slightly behind the hand," Rémy assured us. "I must not be in retard to enflame the noon cannon."

Chadwick watched him go and seemed to brood for a time on something yet unspoken.

"About all that getting married business, Anty," she finally said. "You think you could live with a wife with a glass eye? In Kensington?"

"But, you don't have a glass eye."

"Not yet, I don't, but I tend to live life close to the edge. You may need to habituate yourself to a fencing scar and tattoos of a maritime theme, as well."

"Doubtless next season eyepatches and anchor tattoos will be essential accessories for London's smart set."

The midday cannon boomed cordial accord and Chadwick and I tapped our glasses together and drank to the health of breezy banter.

"At the very least, you'll have to leave off defrauding the casinos of the *Cote d'Azur* — do you have any idea what it means if you're caught?"

"We'd have to give the money back?"

"No... well, yes, probably that too," I considered. "But it also means the blackening of the Boisjoly name."

"Hmm, yes, I can see how that's probably already something of a burden."

"You can't imagine my sorrows," I grieved. "But worse than that, it would mean that Mama would return to London, specifically to Kensington. Can you see yourself arguing with that stone-faced wraith over which of you gets to darn my socks?"

"I cannot see that, no."

"Well, there you go."

"You know my mother's terms, Anty." Chaddy took a dramatic sip of champagne and mango. "Figure out how we're doing it, and we'll stop."

"Fair enough." I countered with an equally dramatic sip. "I'm halfway there already."

"No, you're not. You have no idea how we're doing it."

"That's true," I admitted. "I don't. However I was referring to the other mystery — I've solved the murder of Malandrino the Magnificent."

Even if it's me saying so, I have rather a good deal more experience of making announcements of that nature than do most people. There are probably hundreds of perfectly normal chaps — quite bright and given every opportunity in life — who nevertheless never declare they've solved a murder even once, while by then I'd done it, counting this occasion, more than that.

I'm used to a bit of, I don't want to say accolades, but a certain degree of electric drama. Some 'ooh's and 'aah's and 'don't be an ass's, and indeed Chaddy was quite forthcoming, generous in fact. She even deigned to look a bit impressed. The problem wasn't the audience at all, in fact, it was the upstaging by Rémy, who rushed back onto the terrace.

"Anty..."

"Oh, what ho, Rémy, all out of braked ham?"

"Oh, no Anty, this is another pair of sleeves entirely." Rémy regarded us with wide-eyed, Harold-Lloyd, runaway-train awe. "It is Monsieur Max Minefield — he has been murdered."

CHAPTER FIFTEEN

The Multitude of Motives for the Mystifying Murder of Max Minefield

If it hadn't been for the dead body in the water, I'd have believed myself at the composition of something by Monet.

At the centre of the swimming cove, which shimmered a cool indifference, was the little rowboat, complete with shivering biddies. In the water between boat and shore was the unmistakable form of Max Minefield, floating face down.

Even as the biddies rowed themselves ashore and supported each other to their rooms, big, pudgy, purple clouds gathered overhead as if drawn by the singular scene of a silenced circus critic. They jostled for room and bumped into one another, spilling tips and taps of rain. Pilque was sent for to recover the body and this sparked the curiosity of some of the larger, more serious storm clouds who until then had managed to remain aloof. Word spread. Great, overfed cumulus rolled down from the mountains. Robust, roust-about, seafaring cirrus gambolled in on the surf. Together they shoved and cajoled and conspired with mischievous, local-area nimbostratus.

I trotted down to the marina beneath maroon skies and what had become big, sloppy, splashy drops and awaited Pilque's arrival. We secured Max Minefield, lonely in death as in life, in the dry-dock boathouse, and put a sail over him. Then Pilque set about striking his mast and generally securing his boat, until I reminded him that someone would need to go ashore and alert the authorities.

Pilque agreed that someone should do that, but that whoever it was should have two qualities that he felt he lacked — this person should be foolhardy and expendable. The fisherman drew my attention to the horizon and a wide white wall of torrential rain, bearing straight towards the island. Behind it, whipping it onward, cracked lithe limbs of lightning. Already the sea was kicking up white waves and the always-present whirlpools that surrounded the island were spinning high-speed express chutes to the depths.

Pilque elected to monitor weather conditions from the café bar and I dashed, with all the dignity afforded to those who choose to outrun storms in banana-coloured blazers, to the casino. I clattered through the door just as the cliffside of rain, like a block of solid water, subsumed the island. The glass dome of the casino became a humming parabola, amplifying the will of the storm. It wasn't even the steady drumbeat of the tropical tempest — it was a sustained rush, a toneless insistence that 'everyone should pipe down and listen to me, for I am a storm.'

This simple line of thinking was soon backed up by levin flashes and full-throated thunder — not the rumbly, grumbly, growly sort of distant thunder that menaces from the safety of its own yard, but barking, biting, directly-overhead thunder with a score to settle.

Everyone responds differently to crisis, and the casino was a full collective display of degrees of composure. The biddies were at the bar, anguishing over warm brandies, served by Rémy, who was fretting and flitting as bartender. Jacqueline and Chadwick were at the roulette table, engaging Monsieur Roquebrune in casual conversation, punctuated intermittently by indulgent laughter. Mama was holding solemn court at the baccarat table and Deebee was donating to her retirement fund. The commodore was there, as well, but using the playing surface exclusively as support for two elbows and a neat whisky.

The casino, which relied on the skylight for illumination during the day, was dark as night, but a particularly well-timed flash of lightning brought a certain gravitas to the final syllable when I announced, "Max Minefield has been murdered."

I think it's likely they knew it already, and it's not as though I expected much in the way of gnashing of teeth and rending of raiments, but a little respectful dismay might have been in order. On reflection, I should probably count it lucky no one prompted "hip hip…"

As it was, everyone turned a blank look on me with little more than the noncommittal curiosity that regulars lend a stranger entering a pub on a slow night.

"Right, well, continue remaining calm, if you can," I said. "We won't be able to alert the authorities until there's a break in the storm." The storm, at this juncture, rumbled an advisory — this might be a while. "In the meantime, I'll need to question each of you with regard to your movements over the last few hours."

This proposal was met with a collective effective shrug. I began with the biddies at the bar.

"Poor Mister Minefield…" lamented Mimpley.

"…so unloved, so unloveable," clarified Biddicomb.

"But to go like that…" abhorred Mimpley.

"…is just unconscionable," qualified Biddicomb.

"He appears to have been shot," I said. "Once. Economically and expeditiously, from very close range."

The biddies nodded sadly.

"Did you see who did it?" I asked.

The ladies looked at each other curiously, and then at me more curiously still.

"Why, of course, Mister Boisjoly…" said Mimpley with an ominously unequivocal tone.

"…he shot himself," continued Biddicomb in the same vein.

"Shot himself?" I marvelled. "Are you quite sure? There are a number of factors that strongly suggest otherwise, not the least of which is the fact that Max Minefield loved none so well as he loved himself. And how did he manage? He was shot through the heart. Not impossible, by any means, but hardly the path of least resistance you'd expect from someone who'd given up all hope."

"Oh, we didn't see it…" admitted Mimpley.

"…but it's the only way it could have happened," contended Biddicomb.

"He was in the cave, overlooking the cove…"

"…and he was all by himself…"

"…alone, you see. Then we heard a gunshot…"

"…we thought it was the midday cannon, at first…"

"…and it was, in fact, but he must have shot himself at the same instant…"

"…that Rémy fired the cannon."

"Then how did he wind up in the water?" I asked.

"He walked out of the cave…"

"…holding his heart…"

"…then he just fell…"

"…into the sea."

"And the gun?"

"He must have dropped it…"

"…in the cave."

Rémy arrived on the other side of the bar with a squid cocktail which, he somehow assumed, was my usual.

"Rémy, there's a gun in the cave at the swimming cove," I said. "It'll need to be recovered."

"But Anty." Rémy held up empty hands to mime, I believe, empty hands. "I am chocolate. We have been to this cave and there is nothing. Not a gun. Not a thing. It makes the white cabbage."

"Could someone have removed it?"

"Oh, no, Mister Boisjoly…" assured Mimpley.

"…we were right there on the water until you arrived," reassured Biddicomb.

"Then Mister Minefield can't have shot himself," I pointed out. "You're quite certain you saw no one."

"Oh, we saw someone…" corrected Mimpley.

"…but he didn't shoot Mister Minefield," clarified Biddicomb.

"Perhaps he saw who did. Who did you see?"

"Beano," chorused the biddies.

"The Astounding Bounding Bean?"

"No…" modified Mimpley.

"…Beano," bettered Biddicomb.

"Same product, new label," I said. "You're sure it was him? You were some distance out."

"Oh, yes, we've seen him perform many times," claimed Mimpley.

"You can't really miss his curls…" reclaimed Biddicomb.

"…or his moustache…" exclaimed Mimpley.

"…or his stilticycle," declaimed Biddicomb.

"That certainly checks the boxes," I agreed. "What was he doing?"

"He went into the cave with Mister Minefield…" replied Mimpley.

"…but he came out before the gunshot," ensued Biddicomb.

Mimpley and Biddicomb synchronised their nodding agreement with this exoneration, and a nearby lick of lightning impressed itself upon the stained glass roof and projected through it, onto the casino floor, reverse images of Queen Victoria emerging from the foam and composing *Beowulf.*

This added an unexpected fanfare to the arrival, in the same instant, of the Astounding Bounding Bean, who presented at the interior doors in a red-sequined tuxedo. He paused for a surgical dramaturgical beat — precisely long enough for applause to die down, had there been any — and sailed across the casino to the baccarat table. I made my excuses to the ladies, plucked up my ink pot, and joined him.

"What ho, fellow mourners." I sat next to Mama, such that I might assume some of the awesome authority of Bank. "Killed any good critics lately?"

"You must know that the Astounding Bounding Bean didn't do it," assumed the Beano.

"Must I?" I asked. "If you could just refresh my memory…"

"I was led to understand that he was shot," said the Beano coolly. "Obviously, if I were to kill Minefield, it would be with my bare hands."

"I'd have shot him," offered Deebee. "Twice, time permitting."

"Yes, very well," conceded Beano. "If time was a factor then I suppose I might have shot him. Ten thousand francs, please, dealer." Beano counted out a stake from his wallet.

"I think I'd have poisoned him, all things being equal," mused the commodore. "One of those slow-acting toxins you read about — from the spines of the sub-tropical hedge-hog, for instance — so that he could reflect on his sins."

"You overestimate the man, Commodore," opined Deebee. "Knowing Minefield, he'd use the time to criticise your technique in print."

"But you were the last to see him alive," I pointed out to Beano.

"The killer was the last to see him alive," corrected the acrobat. "Who's Bank?"

"Five thousand," said Mama, and Beano matched it. She dealt him a flat and a five, and she gave herself a five.

"But you did meet Minefield today at the swimming cove," I persevered.

"Yes." Beano spoke distractedly while peeking at his card. "No doubt the biddies told you that."

"They did. They recognised you by your distinctive mode of transport."

"I had been at the square, synchronising my act with the bugler." Beano squared off against Mama. He glanced at his five, and then back at Mama. Then he said, "No card."

This would be normal for baccarat, unless Beano's other card was a ten or a face card, in which case he would have only five. If he had six or seven, then drawing another card wouldn't be an option. Eight or nine and he would have a 'natural' and would turn over his cards. Any less than five and he would be required to draw a card. When one's cards total five, in baccarat, one has that which occurs only very rarely in the game — a choice in the matter. Beano had given it some thought, suggesting that he had either a five or a very cool head for baccarat, particularly when Bank is someone like my mother.

Mama, as is typical of her species, betrayed no emotion, but turned over her cards without taking another. She had a queen and a five, for a total of five.

Beano turned over his remaining card; an ace, for a total of six. He had bluffed out my mother.

"Another game?" asked Beano.

"I believe I'll retire as Bank for the evening," said Mama. She slid the shoe to me with all the solemn gravity of a tribal elder stepping out onto an ice floe.

"Right oh, Mumbly, I'll take it from here. Ten thousand?"

"Banco," declared Beano.

I immediately dealt Beano a natural nine and myself baccarat or, as it's known at the Juniper, a 'Boisjoly'. I pushed another stack of ten plaques onto the table and Beano matched it. I dealt him a mystery and a nine, and myself a five and a king.

I would have to draw, but I thought I'd give Beano back a bit of what he gave Mama.

"What made you suddenly decide to visit the cove during rehearsals, Astounding?"

"There was nothing sudden about it." Beano casually looked at his face-down card. "Minefield arranged to meet me there."

"I thought you hated the man."

"Everyone hated Max Minefield, but he claimed that he had momentous news for me. Information that would change my life. Are you going to draw?"

"I'm reflecting. I'm cripplingly indecisive. What was this information that Minefield had to tell you?"

"More of his amateur sedition," scorned Beano. "He told me

that he had it on good authority that I was to be pushed out of the circus."

"What?" boomed Deebee. "He said that? I'll kill him."

"He said that you told him yourself," Beano said to Deebee with unaffected indifference.

"Well, I didn't."

"Of course you didn't," acknowledged Beano. "But he gave me five hundred thousand francs as a signing bonus to join his ridiculous high-wire musical."

"You took it?" Deebee was aghast. "You signed on with him?"

"Naturally I signed on with him," said Beano. "He gave me five hundred thousand francs, and it's not as though he was ever going to get backing for *Trapezy Peasy*. Have you heard any of the songs?"

"He has a point," I agreed. "It's appalling."

"Now will you draw?" asked Beano.

I gave myself a six, for a total of one. Beano turned over a seven, for a total of six.

"I claim Bank," said Beano, and I slid him the shoe.

There's little difference between Bank and Punter in baccarat except for one rather pivotal privilege — Bank decides how much actual dosh is at stake.

"Fifty thousand." Beano bought five, ten thousand franc plaques from the dealer. "Takers?"

We looked first to Deebee, who smiled serenely and kept his money in his pocket. Next was the commodore who said, quite reasonably, "Do you even want me in your camp?"

Mama stared straight ahead, thinking of her younger, hungrier days. I turned the icy eye of offended filial fidelity on Beano, and bought fifty thousand foolish francs.

"Is this where all the drama is unfolding tonight?" Chadwick took the place next to Beano.

"Clearly not." Jacqueline shored up my left flank, with Mama on my right. "There are barely a hundred thousand francs on the table. Can you even buy anything these days for a hundred thousand francs?"

Beano smiled a cool, collected, performer's smile and dealt me a five face down and a ten. He gave himself a nine.

My default strategy, in the absence of the obvious, is to do nothing at all. Baccarat is almost entirely composed of obvious moves but here I had the choice of trying to improve on five, which is the smart thing to do when Bank is showing anything over four, or staying with my default strategy.

I remained still and stoic. Jacqueline lit a cigarillo and created a low-lying pressure front over the table. Chadwick laughed at something esoteric and unknowable — one of those scintillating titters that pretty women use to make a chap feel like a little boy holding a bouquet of wilted wildflowers — and she set a flickering coin spinning on the table. Mama raised the corner of my five and glanced at it, offered me the slightest and wryest of slight and wry smiles, and put the card back down.

Beano's brow flickered. His forehead produced a single but significant drop of perspiration. He drew a card. An eight. He turned over his remaining cards; a six and a nine, for a total of three to my five.

"You're welcome," moaned the commodore. "You see," he explained to Chadwick, "if I'd bought in, the players would have lost by some heretofore undiscovered number, and the table probably would have caught fire."

"Yes, thanks for that, Commodore," I said. "Incidentally, did you see anything remarkable around the time of the midday cannon?"

"I was in my room," he said. "In my bath. I'd fallen in the sea, if you'll recall."

"Fair enough. Aunt Jacqueline? Where were you at noon today?"

"At noon?" She expelled a confounded cloud. "Where else would anyone be at noon? I was in bed with a good book and a bottle of champagne."

"Very civilised," I approved. "Mama?"

"I dined in my room," Mama said meaningfully. "I had

intended to take lunch on the terrace, but you were there with Chadwick, and I reasoned that you preferred to be alone."

"Sound thinking, I admit, but you're going to need to get to know one another soon enough," I said. "And finally, Deebee — where were you at noon today?"

"On the beach, of course."

"And the biddies were on the water. Rémy was on cannon duty. The hotel staff, we can presume, were staffing the hotel. If everyone's telling the truth…" I paused as a crack of lightning projected Victoria's famously censorious eyebrows onto the baccarat table. "Indeed, even if everyone's trading in artisanal porky pies — we have another impossible murder."

This sort of announcement often has a dampening effect on conversation. For a moment we sat around the baccarat table listening to the rain.

"Deebee," I asked, suddenly recalling an important cast member, "what were you doing on the beach?"

"Getting things ready for tomorrow," he answered with faint reproach. "You ever execute an elephant before? You wouldn't believe how much there is to do."

"You weren't weatherproofing Thumpy's cage or… something?"

"Weatherproofing? How do you weatherproof an open-topped elephant cage?"

"Do you mean to tell me that Thumpy's outside? In the storm?"

Deebee shrugged, lightning flashed, thunder crashed, and the rain dashed down in torrents.

CHAPTER SIXTEEN

Dread, Dismay and Danger, and a Banana-Coloured Blazer

I charged outside into what can best be described as a solid block of wet, and I thought of fives. And mornings. And all those other uncountable moments throughout the day when one is confronted with choice — usually inconsequential but ofttimes capable of giving the course of human events a first-class corker to the back of the head.

Most baccarat hands are aided by a rigorous absence of options. For mornings, I have Vickers.

That doesn't eliminate the decision, of course, it merely narrows it from multiple choice to true-or-false — should I or should I not trust Vickers' judgement today. He doesn't get it universally right, is the problem, and stumping for Vickers on one of his fluffier days is how I get turned away from Epson on the grounds of paisley golf trousers or end up answering a charge of being in control of an unlicensed hansom cab in Burlington Arcade without my false whiskers.

This morning, to be fair, he had defended his thesis; 'The serge,' he had said, 'is better suited to the weather'. Serge is a tight cross-weave, and it maintains a stiff British resolve under trying conditions to the point that it's used to make the sort of trench coats that actually see the inside of trenches.

Conversely, banana-coloured linen blazers' response to the slightest moisture is to shrink into tight restraints. I tried to remove it but it was already too late — my arms were pinned to my sides and I moved as if I were carrying two heavy suitcases. As I ran with all the grace of a wind-up duck, passing the swimming cove, I saw that the sea and air had merged into a sort of churning, turning, hurling shout made manifest in wet weather. Even the path ahead was obscured by sheets of white rain, but when I entered the deep, damp green of the jungle the torrents filtered through the canopy of palm fronds into spouts — a thousand full-force spigots turned the hilly trail ahead into a sleek, slick, slippy landslide that, were I twelve years old or less pressed for time, I'd have made rather a day of. But Thumpy was suffering who knows what torments under the full force of merciless elements that give no quarter for sensitive souls.

As it was, I lost my footing at the first turn and tobogganed the rest of the way down the hillside. Constrained by what amounted to a very efficient straightjacket, I relied on the branches and tree trunks to slap me in the face and kick me in the haunches and gently guide me along my path. I hit the banks with such velocity that, with a squishy bounce off a convenient boulder, I vaulted into the water. When I came out, I avow, I was drier than when I went in.

I struggled to my feet under the burden of a banana-coloured blazer that now weighed more than I did and yet was smaller by about two child sizes. I slipped over the rocks to the beach and learned in an instant another valuable lesson in zoology that would have served me enormously ten minutes earlier — elephants like the rain.

I've since recounted this to a number of acquaintances who reply — to a man — with a casual, retrospective expertise; 'Of course', they'll say professorily, 'everybody knows that.' Well, I mean to say, they're wrong right out of the gate — I didn't. I'd heard that cows will typically ask to be let back inside at the first sign of poor golfing weather and I had an aunt who had a pomeranian that would bark and howl at a storm until it stopped, a service for which he expected to be compensated. I was going by that.

Thumpy, however, was communing with the storm in much the same spirit with which a puppy communes with a ball of wool. He had tamped down a sizable section of the floor of his cage to create an ingenious, impromptu pond, and he was pouncing on it with his front thumpers to create immense splashes which very nearly emptied the pool. Then with wide-eyed delight he would watch it fill in again, draw half of it into his trunk, and then fountain it directly overhead, compounding the rainfall.

He was bounding around in circles, kicking up his and legs blowing bubbles, when he spotted me and stopped. Our eyes met and I fancy he felt he'd been caught by an adult, but a moment later he went right back to splashing about.

The beach had been transformed since my last visit. What had been an unidentifiable chaos of equipment and apparatus was now a full three-ring circus, formed around Thumpy's cage. The second ring was mainly composed of lumps under canvas but at the centre of the first was a tall, narrow scaffold, stretching up almost the height of the elephant cage. Near the top was a platform and from that a steel cable extended out to sea and disappeared into the fog. Beyond that, presumably, was anchored Little Miss Fortune, and indeed I could hear beneath the storm the low churning of steam pistons. At the bottom of the scaffold were tools of the tight-rope trade — poles and bicycles and unicycles and a kitchen chair and a rocking chair. I think there may have been an upright piano, too, but it was under a tarpaulin and difficult to identify with any certainty.

Snaking out of the water were two fat, oily cables, curving and coiling up the beach to a theatrically big red button, as described by the commodore. There was another characteristic, in addition to the theatricality and bigness and redness of the button that didn't quite sit with the commodore's description, and it didn't strike me until my attention was drawn to it by a little spark. Something within the contraption crackled and snapped and spat out a puff of smoke — the thing was plugged in and live. The button was positioned next to the cage and I saw, to my horror, that it was further connected to a metal plate, partially submerged in Thumpy's wading pool.

Another spark, larger this time, was followed by another larger still. The rain was flooding the big red button box and would soon complete the circuit, and Thumpy would be electrocuted.

"Thumpy, get out of the water." I tried to express this with some authority, but as I was constrained to flail like a banana-coloured penguin I failed to express the urgency of the situation, and Thumpy only replied with a happy tantara on his built-in horn section.

I lost sight of all but the button, now only feet away but spitting sparks and smoke and sudden death. The cables were attached by immense sockets, the size of champagne bottles, and restrained as I was, I couldn't get a grip on one. A sustained, fizzing, sizzling, serial spark filled me with the dread of ten Boisjolys. I expanded my chest and shoulders and a great rending of seams was heard — the banana-coloured blazer had no further hold over me. I seized the socket but in that same instant water spilt over the button case, the circuit was made, and the wires buzzed with living and lethal electricity. Thumpy trumpetted a last, agonising clarion call, and was silent.

I raised my eyes from my leaden failure and saw Thumpy balancing on his big rubber ball, safely out of the reach of a tiny, tawny mouse that peered at him from the bale of hay.

I disconnected the theatrically big red button of death and threw the cables into the sea.

"Thumpy the elephant is safe, Vickers," I said from the scalding comfort of my cauldron bath.

"I'm very gratified to hear that, sir," replied Vickers with that flat, formal inflexion he reserves for occasions when he has no idea what I'm talking about. "More hot water?"

"Please," I said. "And a hot whisky, if you can squeeze anything out of the canteen."

I revisited my underwater kingdom again briefly and when I returned to the surface world Vickers handed me a toddy and the following trailing accolade, "...and saved the elephant from electrocution."

"Why, yes, that's exactly what happened." I inhaled my whisky and bath vapours and appreciated, once again, the indoors. "How did you come to know that?"

"I surmised as much from your announcement."

"What an uncanny thing," I boggled. "Although to give credit where it's due, it was mainly the tireless work of a tauny-coloured mouse."

Vickers regarded me with that baffled, judgemental gaze I see so often from Bow Street magistrates when I try to lighten the atmosphere with a limerick. "Do I understand you to say that a mouse has determined how Malandrino was killed?"

"Ah, I think we've failed to achieve a perfect meeting of minds, Vickers. There you are over on the platform for the Murder Express, while I'm here awaiting the Death By Accident Omnibus. Although you're still not far off the truth — I do know how Malandrino was killed, and it was a most sinister and uncanny plot indeed, requiring the tightly coordinated actions of two parties."

"One of whom was a mouse, sir?" Vickers spoke with uncharacteristic incredulity — he normally effects to believe almost anything.

"No, not a mouse," I said. "However a mouse was instrumental in the solution. Incidentally, did you know that elephants are afraid of mice?"

"I understand that to be the widely held view, sir, yes."

"Oh, right, well, confirmed," I said. "But did you also know that they're very *not* afraid of tempests? The more tempestuous the better, in fact."

"Yes, sir."

"You never did."

"I believe I did," Vickers deftly differed. "I expect the phenomenon is a matter of common knowledge."

"I'll bet it isn't," I said. "In fact, Vickers, when we're back in London, I will share this epiphany with some of the more worldly members of my club and I'll wager you anything you'd care that they'll all be just as surprised as I was."

"Very good, sir."

"In any case, good job I didn't know that, or I wouldn't have gone to rescue Thumpy from the storm and finish up rescuing him from accidental execution. And I wouldn't be in this warm tub, solving the murder of Max Minefield," I said. "By the way, Vickers, Max Minefield has been murdered."

"So Mrs Boisjoly has given me to understand, sir."

"You've invited Mama here for cocktails, as requested, then?"

"Yes, sir," confirmed Vickers. "Along with Mrs and Miss Quillfeather."

"Excellent. And the police?"

"The storm, if anything, has grown more intense since your return, and has been joined by gale-force winds," reported Vickers, meteorologically. "Monsieur Pilque remains unable to go ashore."

"Then it's down to me to solve these mysteries three 'ere the sun rises again," I said. "Lay out our finest ermine cape, Vickers, or saddle-blanket poncho or whatever you deem fit for prevailing weather conditions. I'm entirely in your hands, just as the future of the *Cirque d'Azur,* the Boisjoly name from Marseilles to Monte Carlo, and the very life of Thumpy the elephant are entirely in mine."

Thus it was moments later I was getting on the other side of the navy serge double-breasted and explaining to Vickers, "Of course, Minefield's demise is another impossible murder."

"I would have assumed."

"Safest bet, when we're on hand, isn't it," I agreed. "First, he was shot with a gun which cannot have left the scene of the crime and yet which cannot be found. Second, he was seen entering a cave — a cave with a clear line of sight from the bathing cove and no other egress — by the biddies, who also corroborate the claim of The Astounding Bounding Only Viable Suspect that he entered the cave, met with Minefield, and left him most definitely — and most unfortunately, in the view of a uniform majority of those who knew him — alive."

"I hesitate to state what appears to be the obvious, sir, but could the testimony not be reversed?"

"You mean that Beano may be unknowingly providing the biddies with a false alibi," I inferred. "I thought of that, but the ladies were in turn seen by Rémy, when he fired the midday cannon, and they were in the water."

"Midday, sir?" Vickers gazed in the rough direction of the balcony doors and beyond, into the fog and forment of yester-hour.

"Something strikes you as noteworthy about the time of day, Vickers?"

"I was on the balcony, sir, when the cannon was fired." Vickers spoke this with a sort of bewildered surprise at the clarity of the recollection.

"Today, Vickers?" I asked. "I remind you that you were here with my parents twenty years ago."

"I recall it distinctly," claimed Vickers. "I had left the papers on the balcony to dry, and when I went to retrieve them, they were gone."

"Gone! Great Guildenstern's Garters, Vickers, what's become of them?"

"I have since recovered the papers, sir, but the peculiar circumstance of their disappearance left me with a clear recollection of my movements from midday, when the cannon was fired, and for two or three subsequent hours while I searched the balcony."

"You searched a balcony for two hours?"

"I intermittently forgot what it was that I was looking for," said Vickers. "But I have since recovered the papers."

"Where were they?"

"On the balcony, where I left them. I had failed to recall that the suite has two balconies."

"Ah," I acknowledged. "Did you happen to notice anything?"

"It may be more pertinent to note that which I did not," said Vickers. "I heard no gunshot."

"No, you wouldn't have," I said. "According to the timing and testimony of the biddies and the Bean, it must have coincided with the cannon being fired. Having said that," I reflected, "you apparently wouldn't have heard it anyway. After he was shot, Minefield staggered out of the cave and fell into the water. The biddies claim they were in particularly fine screaming voice and of course they let fly. Rémy didn't hear them and neither did I, on the terrace."

"Nor did I."

"Rémy says that the cove is a sound sink — in fact he calls it a 'hearing washbowl', but I'm gaining a foothold on his approach to English — owing to its peculiar shape, which also dampens the currents that otherwise stir around the island, threatening to unscrew it."

"Then taking all accounts at face value, no one could have murdered Mister Minefield," concluded Vickers. "Have you another tack to take?"

"I have," I boasted, emptily. "I plan to eliminate, one-by-one, everyone who had a motive to murder the critic. You didn't do it, did you Vickers?"

"No, sir."

"You see? We're off to an excellent start already. That leaves only everyone else on the island."

"Surely not the hotel staff."

"He didn't strike me as a generous tipper," I opined. "But no, we can probably exonerate the staff, leaving, in no particular order, the biddies, who may believe Minefield responsible for the death of the man they both loved, assuming they didn't kill him themselves. That could hold true for Mama and, for that matter, Digby and Beano, who also had professional gripes against the man, as did the commodore."

"And Mrs and Miss Quillfeather?"

"Chadwick, never. Her mother, in a heartbeat. And we already know that they were keeping rather explosive secrets — who knows what Jacqueline might do to protect them."

"We are not proceeding, then, under the assumption that the same individual is responsible for both deaths," presumed Vickers.

"Not necessarily," I said. "In any case take note — the death of Malandrino was the result of carefully timed actions by two different parties."

There was a light but eloquent knock at the door, and Vickers opened it to present, ordering from annoyance to flamboyance, Mama, Chadwick, and Jacqueline.

"What ho, criminal underworld," I greeted as the ladies improved the atmosphere. "I regret we have little to offer, in terms of Scottish inspiration…"

"If I may, sir," interjected Vickers. "I fancy there's a bottle of Glen Glennegie '19 in the false bottom of our bootbox."

"One of dear Papa's infinite Easter eggs?" I guessed.

"Yes, sir."

"Scotch and sibilation all round, then, Vickers," I bade. "And if we run out, break open the hat boxes. Please, ladies, be seated. I trust you all know why you're here."

"Well, we think we do," Chaddy sat next to her mother on the divan, across from Mama. "But you won't get the same story out of any two of us. Mum thinks we're going to discuss your participation in the syndicate…" Mama, at this point, inhaled sharply, and Chaddy acknowledged her with a smile and a nod. "...Aunty Cleo thinks you're going to shut it down, and I think we're here because this room has all the whisky on the island."

"And you're all completely correct," I said to Chaddy. "Particularly you."

Jacqueline lit a cigarillo. "The arrangement, Anty dear, was that if you didn't figure out how we're bilking the house, you'd join up."

"And if I did, you'd shut it down."

"Well?"

"You'll have to shut it down."

"You haven't worked it out," doubted Jacqueline.

"Of course I have."

"You'll have to shut it down in any case," said Mama. "Do you know what would become of the family name if it was discovered that one of us was cheating the casino?"

"You need have no concern about that, Mama," I assured her. "Jacqueline isn't your cousin. She's not even a Quillfeather — she and Chadwick are imposters and confidence tricksters."

"Anty," Chadwick pointedly pouted. "You disappoint me."

"It doesn't make me love you any less, Chaddy my dear," I said. "But it does send up a flare or two. For instance, Malandrino knew that you were swindling Deebee Digby, didn't he?"

CHAPTER SEVENTEEN

A Swindle of a Scam
of a Flimfam of a Sham
(With a Little Fiddle of a Plan)

The wind whistled symphonically through the variegated wrought-iron railings of the balconies, and the rain punished the windows and glass doors and reduced exterior visibility to a frenzied white wash.

"We were not swindling Deebee Digby," said Jacqueline with cool detachment, which she accentuated with a long, lazy plume of cigarillo exhaust.

"Oh, no?" I countered, arching a Holmesian eyebrow.

"We weren't, Anty," said Chadwick. "We were swindling Malandrino."

"Quite sure?" I asked. "I'm far from an expert in your select and selective profession, but isn't it a simple common-sense rule that your marks, as I believe you call them, should have something to steal?"

"Malandrino did have something to steal," answered Chaddy.

"Operative word being 'did'." Jacqueline smoked while waiting for a crack of thunder to yield the floor. "He managed to get himself murdered before we could take it from him."

"I see." I spoke with something approaching the chronic sarcasm of the late-stage Latin master. "Then what was all this potted piffle about Prince Louis of Monaco in aid of, if not syphoning away some of Deebee Digby's public relations budget?"

"You can hardly expect us to pay for our own hotel room," objected Jacqueline. "Besides, Louis and I really are great friends."

"Very well." I assumed the bearing of an amalgam of the King's Counsels of my acquaintance and addressed the court. "I see that to extract the truth we will have to resort to the cold, hard pliers of empirical evidence. Vickers?"

"Yes, sir?"

"The photograph, please, Vickers," I prompted.

"Photograph, sir?"

"Yes, the photograph. Of Prince Louis."

"Ah, yes, of course, the photograph." Vickers opened the album and withdrew the item in question.

"Apologies," I explained as I received the picture. "We've had little time to rehearse." I held up the photograph. "Can you identify these people?"

"Of course," said Jacqueline idly. "That's dear Louis in the middle, with Grand Prix drivers Billy Williams, Rudy Caracciola, and René Dreyfus.

"I'm particularly interested in the identities of the ladies present."

"That would be Yvonne Aupicq, Chou-Chou, and Charlotte."

"And who did Deebee Digby think they were?"

"He never saw the picture," answered Jacqueline, "but if you read the inscription on the back, you'll see that Malandrino would have thought that Chou-Chou and Charlotte were Jacqueline and Chadwick Quillfeather."

I turned the picture over.

"There is no inscription on the back."

"I can't help that," offhanded Jacqueline.

"Doubtless it was washed away during its time in the water," suggested Vickers. "This was a recurring eventuality during your father's time. Eventually it proved necessary to embroider the address labels in his hats and coats."

"Who wrote your assumed names on the back of the photograph?" I asked.

"I did." Jacqueline spoke as though stating the obvious and then, to polish the point, added, "obviously."

"Why?"

"So that Malandrino would think that we were imposters."

"It's called 'the formula', Anty." Chaddy waded in to the rescue. "If the mark thinks he has something on you, then he's more likely to trust you."

"We caused Malandrino to come into possession of the photograph so that he could blackmail us," added Jacqueline.

"Blackmail you?" I queried. "For what?"

"A piece of the action," said Chaddy. "It's how the formula works — the mark thinks he's swindling us."

"Malandrino discovered that we were running a play on Deebee, and he threatened to expose us unless we cut him in," explained Jacqueline.

"So you *were* swindling Deebee," I surmised.

"Only for hotel bills and drinks," said Jacqueline. "And there's always someone who'll pay hotel bills and drinks."

"Deebee thought that he was going to get a concession to run the only fixed circus on the Riviera, in Monte Carlo," continued Chadwick. "We were making all the arrangements, so we knew that the venue would have to be a stretch of recovered land next to the casino."

"The swindle, if I may take a guess, was to buy the land first, and sell it to Deebee at an enormous profit once he'd received the concession from Prince Louis," I said.

"Very good, Anty." Chadwick raised a glass to my scholarship.

"But there is no concession," I reasoned.

"There's not even any land."

"And you were going to sell some of it to Malandrino nevertheless," I said. "How did you know that he wouldn't just expose you to Deebee?"

"A certain talent for judging character is a core skill in our profession," explained Jacqueline.

"Besides, what if he had exposed us?" asked Chaddy. "The picture doesn't prove anything at all, and there's no way of definitively establishing the absence of a Monte Carlo circus monopoly."

"That's…" I began that sentence with a quite fixed idea where it was heading but then immediately hit a fork in the road. "…diabolically cunning. You can't actually get caught."

"This is one of the principal selling features of the formula," said Chaddy. "I recommend it very highly."

"Noted," I said. "But, obviously, when we're married, you'll have to apply your dangerous intellect to higher things. We can't have the children selling counterfeit tickets to Buckingham Palace to tourists."

"Married? Children?" Mama spoke with a, for her, scandalised tone. "What children?"

"Edmond, I think, to honour dear Papa," I replied. "And of course, as a tribute to where we met, little Vicky." Then I added, as an aside to Mama, "She's the one I really worry about."

"You needn't let that trouble you, Anty," said Jacqueline. "Chaddy's already determined to undermine the best of plans with good intentions."

"Oh, mother."

"Well, it's true." Jacqueline spoke gravely. "I can almost not bear to say it — my daughter was going to give the money back."

"Back?" I said. "To Malandrino?"

"To the biddies," said Chadwick. "We met them at Cap Ferrat and we soon worked out the play Malandrino was running on them."

"How anyone can be taken in by that sort, I'll never understand." Jacqueline casually examined her cigarillo.

"Mind you, I don't understand how anyone can be taken in by my sort, either."

"So, you were swindling Malandrino on behalf of the biddies," I speculated in a deliberately dubious tone.

"That was the plan," said Chadwick. "But then he got squashed before we could close the deal."

"Then the biddies will just have to settle for the money you've stolen from the casino," adjudged Mama. "And you'll have to stop."

"No we won't." Jacqueline finished her drink with an 'I'll have another' flourish, and Vickers set about conducting the clinking concerto.

"You will," insisted Mama. "Won't they, Anty?"

"No," I said. "In fact, they won't have to stop cheating the casino, Mama, because they never started."

"Oh, Anty." Chadwick put down her glass to clap approvingly. "I'm so proud of you."

"Never started?"

"You can't cheat a casino," I said. "It can't be done. Much simpler and more practical is to *appear* to cheat a casino, and collect investment capital from a gambling syndicate that believes itself onto a sure thing."

"But... I saw them winning," said Mama.

"You saw Jacqueline consistently come out ahead at roulette," I corrected. "In fact you witnessed a very simple but effective illusion — Jacqueline and Chadwick each bet on black and red, respectively. Whichever came up, they would casually reposition so that Jacqueline stood before the square that appeared to win, but their total take was almost always zero. The croupiers know the ladies are a team, they may even be aware of what they're doing, but it's hardly against the rules to share winnings. To enhance the effect of the spectacle, Chadwick would spin her coin on the table and appear to examine the rotation for fine irregularities."

"But what about *vingt-et-en?*" asked Mama. "Chadwick never failed to leave the table ahead of the game."

"By how much?"

"I don't know, but it must have been a great deal."

"It was a pittance," I said. "Of all table games, though, *vingt-et-un* affords the best odds to the player. Casinos always come out ahead on the day, of course, but in the case of *vingt-et-un* they rely on punters holding out for the big win. Over the course of a modest period of play, at some point everyone will be ahead by some small amount, however briefly. If, when that moment arrives, you take out a coloured monocle and appear to examine the table before taking your winnings and leaving, you win a great deal more than a few thousand francs — you win the awe-struck admiration of your audience."

"But she didn't win small amounts, Anty," persisted Mama. "She always walked away with stacks of chips."

"To which she deftly and discreetly contributed from her reserve of the biddies' investment," I explained. "The penny dropped for me when I realised that I'd accidentally conned the ladies into believing that the waters of Cap Royale are irretrievably polluted with sunken treasure."

"You're not cheating the casino?" Mama spoke to Jacqueline, who smiled and exhaled a smug smog through her nose. "What a relief. Ah, thank you, Vickers."

Vickers moved among us, distributing distilled discussion and water. For a brief period there was calm and camaraderie and a wordless appreciation for the whipping storm only feet away.

"Just a moment." Mama paused her whisky trajectory. "If you're not stealing from the casino, and you're not stealing from the biddies, what's the point of all this theatre?"

"I expect, Mama, that in regular practice, the operation doesn't involve returning the syndicate's money," I suggested.

"That's true," said Chadwick. "Usually the final scene is more along the lines of a quiet departure in the middle of the night."

"But on this occasion, the entire ruse is being performed to allow you to return some of the money that Malandrino took from the biddies without them knowing where it came from," I concluded.

"Gold star, Anty," enthused Chadwick. "That is — or, rather, that was — exactly the plan."

"How much were you expecting to get from Malandrino?" I asked.

"Practically nothing," scorned Jacqueline. "Just four thousand pounds. It's all he had left."

"But it meant the world to the biddies," added Chadwick. "It's the difference between what they have and what they need to buy into the circus."

"Is Deebee willing to sell shares?"

"He thinks he's cheating the biddies, of course," said Chadwick. "After he gets the concession, he'll move his best acts to Monte Carlo and the *Cirque d'Azur* will just be a name."

"So, you see," I said to Mama, "there was never any question of cheating the casino."

"But, you *were* cheating Malandrino," Mama said to Jacqueline.

"Who was cheating the biddies," I added.

"And thought that you were cheating Deebee," continued Mama.

"Who thought he was cheating the biddies," I concluded.

"It sounds so simple when you put it like that," exhaled Jacqueline in a cloud of smoke. "But I assure it was far more nuanced in the execution."

"The chief reason," I said, "why I don't want to explain it all to Rémy. Life is too short for explaining things in French. However, unless my conditions are met, I'll be forced to report you."

"And for what would you report us, Anty?" asked Jacqueline. "Would that be for not cheating the casino? Or would you expose the scandal of not swindling Deebee Digby? Certainly you have the undeniable evidence of a photograph of some people who aren't us."

"Yes, fair point," I conceded. "What about staying at the hotel under false identities?"

Thunder rumbled and Mama, Jacqueline, and Chadwick shared some mute, meaningful message of the sort exchanged between adults before speaking some home truth about Father

Christmas or the dark origins of black pudding.

Mama was somehow nominated spokeswoman. "Anty, this really is Jacqueline and Chadwick Quillfeather."

"I say," I marvelled. "That is playing the long game."

"What's your condition, Anty?" asked Chadwick, mercifully.

"Well, I'm not so sure, now," I faffed. "I was hoping for a confession."

Mama remained after the Quillfeather faction departed, along with Vickers, to whom I assigned discreet duties to be performed elsewhere.

"Well, isn't that jolly?" I said. "You're not only losing a son and gaining a daughter-in-law, you've picked up an extra second cousin by marriage. How long have you known about Jacqueline?"

Mama stood at the broad, glass balcony doors, holding her whisky and facing the lashing storm, like a harpy gazing upon that which she wrought, and adjudging it middling.

"How long have I known what about Jacqueline?"

"Excellent question," I said. "That does appear to be a rather broad field, doesn't it? Take your pick, though what makes me wonder is how it is that Vickers didn't know that I had an Aunt Jacqueline Quillfeather."

"Her marriage to cousin Ambrose was not, for perhaps obvious reasons, widely spoken of in the family," answered Mama.

"Still, not much gets past Vickers up to and including June 22nd, 1911," I observed, "after which everything gets past Vickers. It's my personal pet theory that he's out of space."

"Their marriage was a secret, Anty." Mama spoke in low tones, as though anyone listening could possibly hear her over the roaring storm. "I myself only learned of it a few years ago, when I met Jacqueline for the first time in London."

"And scandal has dogged her heels since," I guessed. "Or, perhaps more accurately, she has doggedly pursued scandal — seems more in keeping with her personality. This is why you were prepared to believe that the Quillfeather cousins were capable of cheating a casino."

"Precisely."

"Well, that clears that up," I said. "But what made you think that little Anty Offspring was any sort of match for them?"

"You told me so."

"I see." I took a sardonic sip of scotch. "So you stand by your risible assertion that you know nothing of my achievements in Blighty."

"Regrettably, Anty, I've largely lost touch with your drunken clubmates."

"So the witness has previously testified," I recalled. "We are to understand that there are cloistered nuns in the mountain regions of Albania with a greater command of world events than you have. You're cut off here on this remote island from all daily newspapers and communication with your late husband's only sister."

"I told you, I haven't seen your Aunt Azalea since your father's funeral," claimed Mama, "and even then she pretended to not recognise me."

"You probably frightened her," I explained. "You frighten everyone."

"Everyone frightens Azalea," parried Mama. "You frightened her, when she first saw you at your christening. So did Vickers, the grandfather clock and your stuffed shrew."

"Anteater. Mister Snaardvark."

"What's all this about you marrying Chadwick?" Mama finally turned her full attention on me.

"You've met the girl," I pointed out. "What possible further explanation could be required?"

"She is a criminal."

"Genius comes in many forms," I agreed. "It will be a trial, at the outset, raising the children in our respective faiths. Doubtless it will give them a more balanced world view."

"Don't be absurd, Anty."

"You're of the prevarication school of parenting, are you?" I asked. "Think that children should be judiciously lied to? Perhaps you're right, but I shall be looking to you for guidance on that. Have you any books to recommend?"

"There is no such book, Anty."

"A thinking woman would call that a gap in the market."

"This is just another of your fancies," claimed Mama. "You've been proposing to girls on a bi-monthly basis since first meeting the neighbour's daughter in Gloucester Gardens."

"Ah, Dottie," I reminisced. "I still maintain I could have made her very happy, had we been allowed out of our prams. This is different, though, Mama. Chaddy is magnificent. She's complicated and compelling and ambiguous and ambitious. She's the pith and pulp of dreams that slip away on waking, made manifest in a single splendid rush. Easy on the eyes, too."

"I assume that you propose to move her into the house in Kensington." Mama turned back to the glass and spoke this assumption to the storm.

"I'd forgotten how long you'd been away," I said. "Yes, it's all the rage, these days, husbands and wives living under the same roof. Chief reasons are largely economical, I expect, but I can see certain practical advantages to the arrangement. Of course, this will be after I've sorted out these three murders — otherwise people won't talk of anything else at the reception."

"What three murders?" asked Mama, idly. "You don't mean your father."

"I do mean my father," I said. "It can wait, what with the more immediate threat to the life of Thumpy the elephant, but it can't wait forever."

"I wish you'd stop thinking of your father's death as murder, Anty," said Mama. "It's in the dead past."

"It is," I agreed. "And the best theory is that it was put there by a professional assassin, hired by someone who knew his habits well, the silver lining being that, at least, he felt no pain."

"He rarely did."

A deep, sustained, moaning monophony rattled the glass. Mama stared it down and, in time, the thunder backed off in favour of uninterrupted rain and black fog that gave the impression that the entire dark stew of stormy sky had descended onto the little island and cut it off from the world.

"That's going to last all night," I noted. "And the police won't be able to get here until morning."

CHAPTER EIGHTEEN

A Menacing Beckoning
to an Unsettling Reckoning

My own imperfect plan was to comport myself exactly as though I was at a casino hotel on the Riviera. After all, only the dead knew what I knew, and the guilty would certainly know that nothing could happen until morning, when everything would happen at once.

The casino, however, was empty. In fact, it was by all appearances closed. There was no staff and the lights were out. I was left with no option, of course, but to set up shop.

With the aid of frequent flashes of turquoise lightning, I fitted out the baccarat table with a candelabra, a bottle of Courvoisier '99, a tray of glasses, and a fully-loaded card shoe.

There's a certain operatic immensity to an after-hours casino which is only compounded by a flaming candelabra and a belting storm. The effect was to make of the baccarat table a cosy, warm, dry, well-lit sanctuary against the nightmare borders all around, beyond which there be monsters.

I fancied I felt eyes upon me as I sat there in the dark. I also fancied I heard the interior casino door open and close, a shuffling sound, someone or something getting shinned on a table leg, and footsteps. The first visual sighting I had of an eerie presence was matching patent leather boots, scintillating in the candlelight at the edges of my refuge. Presently, Deebee

Digby stepped into the clearing.

"What ho, circus mogul," I yelped, for some reason. Casino nerves, I expect.

"Evening, Boisjoly." Deebee approached the table in his three-ring silks, complete with red cummerbund. "Playing against yourself?"

"Everyone has a system," I explained. "I always play the odds. Sniffle?" I poured a generous brandy and topped up my own glass. "Bar staff was a little absent, and so a tactical response was called for."

"I know," Deebee eased with uncharacteristic calm into the opposition position. "I met Rémy earlier. He says the storm put the power out in the casino."

"Of course." I looked around us at the void. "I can see how the empty bar and unmanned tables would follow neatly from that. Card?"

"What'll we play for?"

"Why, sport, Deebee," I said, dealing us each one face down card and, respectively, an eight and a four. "Trial and test. The cut and thrust of instinct and intellect across the green velvet battlefield."

"Natural nine." Deebee turned over an ace.

"Deftly played."

"Let's up the stakes." Deebee drew on his drink as lightning struck his face into aquamarine relief. "How about we play for a measure of plain truth?"

"Oh, ehm, right oh."

"Weren't counting on this storm, were you Boisjoly?"

"You have me well rumbled, Deebee," I admitted. "I was taken entirely by surprise. Completely ruined a banana-coloured blazer and severely traumatised an entirely harmless pair of espadrilles. Incidentally, Deebee — and reflect on this, for I require a full and frank answer — did you know that elephants like wet weather?"

I dealt another hand. Deebee was showing a nine and I was showing a five.

"Natural nine." Deebee turned over a king. "Your fiancée tells me that you've got it all figured out."

"Did she say that?" I asked. "I say, that's nice to hear. I'm not sure that I'd go so far as all that, but it's healthy for a woman to respect her man's world view, don't you think?"

"I mean in regards to Malandrino."

"Ah. She told you that, did she?"

"And Minefield."

"She exaggerates." I waved dismissively and drank defensively. "It's like that with new romance, you know. Chap I know from my club, Dagbert Dewars — we call him Drams, of course, for his own good — met, madly fell for, and proposed to one Felicity Smith-Sootersmith in the space of a single East Sussex village fête, and on return to the metropolis, like most men suffering under the influence, wouldn't and couldn't belt up about her. Above all, though, even surpassing her poise and intellect and — his words, not mine — her fairy-bunny nose, Drams praised Felicity's remarkable singing voice."

"Point being?"

"It's just ahead a bit," I assured him. "You see, Felicity had hit a couple of high As over middling C at this fête — some hunting song as her contribution to the inevitable entertainments — and in the dizzy delirium of new love Drams heard the angels sing. Had common sense and the near unanimous vote of the Juniper billiards committee held any sway, the banns would have been read in the new year and poor Drams would have had a chance to convalesce to something like an objective ear, but as it was the wedding took place that very season and at the reception the groom insisted that the bride let us hear what all the fuss was about. She sang Ave Maria."

"Not good?"

"Depends on what you mean by good," I allowed. "It struck me an uncannily realistic impersonation of a trainload of goats going over lightly damaged points. But, by the classical measure of wedding music, no, not good. The silence that followed haunts my dreams to this day. It's what I imagine the surface of the moon sounds like at an awkward moment. As it happens, the Smith-Sootersmith clan includes no less than two bishops — the wedding champagne was served, still cold, at the annulment party."

"And the point, then, finally?"

"You know, I believe I've forgotten."

"Chadwick exaggerates, you said."

"That's it. She does. She exaggerates. New love, and all that."

"She says that you worked out how Malandrino was killed."

"Ah, that," I said. "That's true, I have done. Card?"

"What's the ante?"

"Another bold truth." I dealt Deebee a seven showing, and myself a nine.

"Natural nine." Deebee turned over a two.

"Good show." I also turned over a two.

"Well? How do you think Malandrino was killed?"

"You don't know?" I asked.

"I have no idea how Malandrino died."

"I know." I took a smug sip of brandy. "Nevertheless, you killed him."

The wind sounded like a sharp intake of breath but then was smothered under a thick layer of thunder.

"I couldn't have," pointed out Deebee. "If you'll recall, like everyone else, I was on board the yacht when it happened."

"And yet you managed to kill him," I said. "Want to know how?"

"Tell me."

"You killed Malandrino by firing him out of a cannon into the cliff above the beach, from whence he fell into Thumpy's cage, displaying all the symptoms of a clown who had been fatally trampled."

"Do you have any idea how cannons work, Boisjoly?"

"In principle. Not very different in function to a champagne cork, I believe."

"The yacht was on the other side of the island."

"No, it wasn't," I said. "That's why you didn't know until just now how you managed to make it look like Malandrino had been trampled to death — you thought that you were shooting him out to sea."

"And why would I do that?"

"To make it appear that he had abandoned you without letting him actually abandon you," I explained. "He either told you that night or, more probably, had already told you that he was quitting the *Cirque d'Azur* to start and star in his own production. He probably didn't mention that he had come into possession of a necklace worth some twenty thousand pounds, but he convinced you that he could manage it."

"Malandrino would never have left me." Deebee spoke with little conviction.

"Malandrino betrayed the woman who loved him and his brothers-in-arms," I pointed out. "He tortured animals, large and small, and he swindled those who admired him most. If it would have benefited him, he'd have sold you for bait."

Deebee shrugged at this plain fact, and took a consoling draw of his brandy.

"You knew that," I continued, "and you feared that a rival show benefiting from Malandrino's fame would cost you your lifetime opportunity — the Monte Carlo circus concession. If you couldn't have him, nobody could. You had to make it look as though he had disappeared, which is why you threw his steamer trunk overboard. This confused the issue considerably, because it was initially assumed that the trunk had been disposed of in order to destroy something that was locked inside it, but you only wanted to make it look as though Malandrino had quietly stolen away in the night. And it might have worked, had the yacht stayed in one place."

"What makes you think it wasn't where everybody — absolutely everybody — on board, said it was?"

"The original idea, to give credit where it's due, came from a wasp."

"What wasp?" scoffed Deebee.

"We aren't well-acquainted," I confessed. "Vickers knows him better, although if truth be known I don't think they get on well. Nevertheless, it was while watching this insect blister towards what he thought, in his sugar-blind inebriation, the world beyond my suite and connecting, instead, with a copper etching of Queen Victoria, that the seed was planted."

"That's absurd."

"It is," I agreed. "You'd think in the rooms, at least, there'd be the occasional landscape, still and all, the best of ideas can come from the rummiest of sources. However, it was Chaddy who turned inspiration into theory when she described standing on the bow of the yacht, watching the mountains disappear into the night. Then I recollected that Max Minefield had been seen watching the sun set from the starboard side. Either of these observations means that at the beginning of the evening Little Miss Fortune was anchored pointing inland. When I arrived, the yacht was facing out to sea, with the starboard side to the east."

Deebee swirled his snifter and observed the resulting waves of brandy, possibly pursuant of some rudimentary experiment which in the end proved inconclusive.

"What does that prove?"

"On its own, nothing, but it promotes the absurd to not only possible but probable," I said. "Malandrino was, I expect, on his way to do some last minute tormenting of Thumpy, just as Minefield and Beano supposed, hence the mouse costume. You rendered him cooperatively unconscious, probably with a blow to the head, and stuffed him into the immense cannon on the port side of the boat, lit a long fuse, and then returned to the bow to watch the fireworks, the sound of which would camouflage the detonation when Malandrino was launched into the sea."

A shivering length of lightning lit Deebee from above, raising his features in high relief — to rather sinister effect, I expect, were Victoria's nose not projected onto his forehead.

"You look sceptical," I observed.

"The yacht was anchored in the harbour." To illustrate this simple claim, Deebee held up his snifter.

"No, in fact, it wasn't," I countered. "That's quite key, actually, to the whole thing. Commodore Wairing raised anchor. It's why he was late starting the fireworks show."

"Why would he do that?"

"You'd have to ask him, to be entirely sure," I guessed. "But it's probably safe to say that he was trying to scuttle his boat. His insurance was nearing an end and, along with it, his last chance to divest himself of Little Miss Fortune — he assumed that the famously treacherous whirlpools, in conspiracy with the reefs, would set him free. Against all odds, the yacht simply orbited the island, returning safely to the harbour but facing the other direction — even the commodore, whom you'd imagine would know better, failed to account for his extraordinarily poor luck."

"You're saying that the yacht floated around the island and nobody noticed?"

"You find that improbable?"

"I do."

"It was very dark," I said. "As Chadwick described the moonless night, prior to the fireworks show, you couldn't tell land from sea. Nobody noticed the movement of the yacht, apart from Mama, whose acute seasickness was unaffected by the absence of light. Although, incidentally, the commodore saw you lighting the fuse."

"He never did," objected Deebee. "It was too dark."

"Precisely," I acknowledged. "In fact, he saw someone lighting something, and assumed he was witnessing Max Minefield's unending quarrel with his cigarette."

"That doesn't prove anything." This simple truth appeared to put Deebee more at ease. He took up his snifter and leaned back in his chair. I dealt us each two cards.

Deebee turned over his cards and declared, "Natural eight."

"Baccarat." I revealed two tens. "Very well, I owe you another plain fact, Deebee — I know that Chaddy told you that I worked out how you killed Malandrino, because I asked her to."

"And why would you do that?"

"Frankly, Deebs, I hoped that you'd try to get away before the police arrived," I admitted. "You're right, I hadn't counted on the storm, and usually by this stage of things the authorities have taken a firm hand. I thought that if you legged it then, in the morning, I could just report my findings and be done with it. It's not too late, you know..." As I said this, a tremendous crash of thunder shook the entire casino. "I think it's letting up."

"And why would I want to leave?"

"Oh, freedom, passion for the open road. You circus types are all filled to tipping with the minstrel spirit, don't you know."

"I mean to say," Deebee leaned on his elbows and smiled a decidedly unsolicitous sort of smile, "why would I need to get away, when you can't prove any of this?"

"Ah, but I can."

"No, you can't. You've just said that the commodore couldn't tell who it was he saw in the dark."

"I did say that, didn't I?" I recalled. "Too late to take it back, I suppose... No, I thought as much. Then I'll have to settle with proving that you murdered Max Minefield."

"And how are you going to do that?"

"By establishing that you're the only person who could have," I replied.

"It's my understanding that according to the biddies the only person who could have done it was Beano."

"The Astounding Bounding Bean," I corrected. "In fact, the biddies' testimony is that he couldn't possibly have done it — they both saw him leave the cave before the gunshot was heard."

"They're mistaken."

"You're right," I agreed. "They are. They actually saw two different Beanos, and heard two different gunshots, but the biddies, who think with one mind, speak with one voice, and observe with one pair of eyes, also testify as one tremendously unreliable witness."

"And what gave you this wild idea?"

"In this instance the inspiration was a shark," I said. "Not a real shark, obviously — they're nowhere near as clever as they're widely thought to be — but an identity I often assume in the bath. On two occasions, while submerged, my man Vickers was addressing me. I surfaced at the right moment to get the wrong end of the stick entirely, but what I thought I heard appeared to be entirely coherent from my perspective, and what I replied made perfect sense to Vickers, but we were having two different conversations. The biddies, who were diving for treasure while you were murdering Minefield, had a similarly stroboscopic perception of events."

"Stroboscopic?"

"Staccato. Inconsistent," I offered. "Like that which happens between the frames in a movie. While one biddy was underwater, the other was observing one Minefield and one of two beans. Both saw Max enter the cave, and a moment later both saw Beano follow, but then when he left, Miss Biddicomb was underwater. Then both were submerged when you entered the cave — riding a unicycle and wearing a clown wig and moustache — but Miss Mimpley resurfaced in time to hear you shoot Minefield. Owing to the unique acoustical properties of the cove, only Miss Mimpley heard the shot, and she assumed that it was the midday cannon because, as far as she was concerned, Minefield was alone in the cave."

"Sitting duck, then," said Deebee. "Anybody could have killed him."

"No, anybody *would* have killed him," I amended. "Only one person could have, because when you left the cave, you were seen by Miss Biddicomb, who moments later heard the midday cannon. Their combined testimony describes Minefield entering the cave, having a meeting with Beano who then leaves the cave, followed by a gunshot timed to coincide with the cannon. Taken separately, though, it becomes clear that there must have been a second Beano, easily disguised to look like the first, and with the background necessary to operate the requisite equipment."

"Doesn't mean it was me, though."

"Narrows the field considerably, though, I think you'll

agree," I said. "Furthermore, there are only two paths which lead away from the cove — one towards the square, the other to the beach. Only one Beano returned to the square, so the other must have gone to the beach, where I subsequently saw a second stilticycle. By your own admission, you were the only one at the beach at that time."

"And why would I decide to kill Minefield now, after all these years?" asked Deebee. "If I didn't kill him after the review of the Brighton show, or the tour of the Midlands, or after he declared our Christmas parade a hazard to public health, I certainly wouldn't kill him today."

"You show rare reserves of restraint, Deebee," I said. "But today Minefield pushed you too far — he was blackmailing you into financing his high-wire musical."

"What makes you say that?"

"Somebody was giving him the money," I explained. "He no longer wanted it from me, and I should have been his last hope. He saw the commodore that night and, later, when I mentioned that you, too, had gone missing from the party, Minefield realised how Malandrino was killed and who did it — and he was using this knowledge to get what he always wanted."

"I wouldn't put it past him."

"No, nor would I," I said. "Indeed, when Minefield first introduced the opportunity to invest in *Trapezy-Peasy* he made it clear that the proposal included a counter-offer to destroy my mother's reputation."

"Maybe that's what got him killed."

"I thought of that, Deebee, I promise. I tried to make it work but was stymied at every turn by the simple fact that Mama cannot ride a unicycle. Between you and me, she can't ride a bicycle, and isn't entirely at her ease in heels. She has vertigo."

Deebee drank slowly from his snifter in a manner that made Courvesier somehow ominous.

"What makes you think the same thing won't happen to you?"

I met Deebee's squint across the table, and gave back as good as I got.

"Because if it did, Deebee, from that moment on your life would be over as you know it. Your existence would become a series of dark dead-ends and whispers in the night. You'd pass the rest of your days, for as many or as few as there might be, changing your name and your appearance, glancing over your shoulder and never spending more than one night in the same place. And, despite these precautions and provisions and privations, you'll nevertheless be caught completely unaware when, like a leopard, Vickers finally strikes. You'd last longer in the den of a hungry lion, Deebee. I can't state that strongly enough."

"I don't need to kill you, Boisjoly." Deebee once again took up his brandy and leaned away from the table with a disturbing confidence. "You're not going to tell anyone what you know."

"I think I will."

"No, you won't," persisted Deebee. "Unless you want to see your mother hang for murder."

CHAPTER NINETEEN
Reckoning at the Riviera Royale

I was fairly certain that I knew what Deebee meant, but I confess I wasn't sure how to reply to it. I wasn't fully, concretely convinced of the matter myself, but I elected to proceed as though I was.

"If you have information regarding my mother's involvement in a murder, Deebee," I said, "you're going to need to speak in specifics. Mama's is a varied and complicated existence — she still hasn't accounted for her movements during the assassination of Rasputin, you know."

"She had your father killed."

"Oh, that." I waved dismissively. "I know. Card?"

"Please." Deebee finished his brandy. "I'll just turn the evidence over to the police when they get here then, shall I?"

I dealt Deebee a nine showing and myself a seven. Deebee turned over another nine for a natural eight, but I turned up a two for a natural nine.

"Looks like I owe you a truth, now, Boisjoly," said Deebee.

I realised in that moment that I didn't believe it, or at any rate that I hoped, finally, that Mama hadn't had a hand in my father's death. In spite of my blasé bravado, it now mattered to me what Deebee had to say.

"Very well, Deebee," I said. "What is it that you think you have to offer?"

"A confession."

"You can't believe a word that woman says," I countered. "You should hear what she told me about Piccadilly Circus."

"Not from your mother," smugged Deebee. "From Jacqueline."

"What has she to do with it?" I asked. "She never knew my father."

"No, but she knows a lot of other people. Princes, dukes, American millionaires, and even, when your mother had need of one, a professional killer-for-hire."

"Once again, Deebee, your sweet, child-like faith is misguided," I said. "Jacqueline's a confidence trickster."

"I know. She and Chadwick were using me to swindle Malandrino."

"Told you that, did she?"

"She did," confirmed Deebee. "She sold you out, Boisjoly, for four thousand pounds."

"There you are — I told you she's not to be trusted."

"I agree." Deebee withdrew a small fold of papers from his inside pocket. "But your mother put her requirements in writing, and Jacqueline kept the letter."

I sat in silence for a moment and listened to the storm, but it had little to say that it hadn't said already and had been saying all night.

"Very well, Deebee." I refilled his glass and then my own. "What do you want?"

"In a minute. Deal us another hand."

I dealt him a six and myself a king. I had a five face down but Deebee didn't immediately check his cards. He just held my gaze and sipped his brandy. Presently, the sound of the casino door opening and closing came to us, followed by delicate but deliberate footsteps. Then Mama stepped into our little circle of light.

It's been mentioned that my mother at her most expressive is less emotive than Nelson's monument at its least, but there was something somehow *more* impassive and cold about her that was, in itself, meaningful — something of a cross between guilt and 'give me a brandy'. I gave her a brandy and she took her place at the head of the table.

"Shall we turn over our cards, Boisjoly?" said Deebee.

I dealt myself a four. Deebee turned over a king for a total of six. I had nine.

"You win another truth," announced Deebee. "I'll let your mother take this one."

Mama let a caustic glare linger on Deebee but he appeared to be armoured. She turned to me.

"You can't let him give that letter to the police, Anty."

"What does it say?"

"Anty, I'm sorry." Mama looked down at her glass. "But you suspected from the beginning that I arranged to have your father pushed in front of that electric tram at Shepherd's Bush. Well, now you know for sure — it's true."

"And Jacqueline?"

"She made all the arrangements," said Mama to her brandy, "but it was my idea, and I paid for it."

"You will, anyway," added Deebee, "if Anty's performance doesn't meet with audience approval."

"Just a minute, Deebee." I held up my 'yield to oncoming traffic' hand and addressed Mama. "What about Chaddy? Did she know?"

"I'm sorry, Anty."

The storm hissed on the roof above. A series of little lightning bolts flickered a fluorescent Queen Victoria across the floor of the casino, followed by a low grumble. I drank and brooded in silence.

"Very well, Deebee," I said at last. "What do you want for that letter?"

"A little showmanship." Deebee attached himself to the table as he would when developing one of his macabre ideas. "First, your mother's going to say that Malandrino left the yacht that night to go and see Thumpy." Deebee turned to Mama. "He put on his mouse costume, and got in a boat, and rowed ashore."

"When was this meant to have happened?" I asked.

"After the fireworks were supposed to start, but before they actually did." Deebee leaned into the idea, now, and over the table. "She was in Malandrino's stateroom anyway, wasn't she? And Malandrino was unconscious in the cannon — they could have been together, so far as everyone else is concerned. It all ties together, see?"

"Like a bundle of dirty laundry," I agreed. "And Minefield? Are you going to ask Mama to say that she saw Thumpy shoot him?"

"That's *your* big moment, Anty." Deebee held onto the table to keep from bouncing out of his chair. "It happened just like you said — Minefield knew that I killed Malandrino, and he blackmailed me for the financing for his dead-end show, *and* he wanted my headline act. I agreed, and he arranged to meet Beano straight away, so I put on the wig and moustache and tights, waited until after Beano left the cave, and then took his place and gave Minefield the big finale he's had coming for years."

"That seems clear enough," I said. "And you want me to explain all that to the authorities."

"You overlooked one thing, Boisjoly — the biddies saw one Beano come and another go, but there's no reason it can't have been the same Beano — you need to convince the police that's what happened, that Beano killed Minefield."

"Very well," I sighed. "Now, if you'll just hand over that letter, we'll have a gentleman's agreement."

"Not yet, Boisjoly, there's one more thing you have to do." A flash of bright, white, sustained light top-lit Deebee like a circus spot. "Tomorrow morning, at the end of the show, you're going to press the button and execute Thumpy."

This was punctuated with a thunderous exclamation point.

"But… Thumpy's entirely innocent," I objected.

"I know it," said Deebee in a disparaging tone, as though innocence rated very low on the list of failings that Deebee Digby could abide in an elephant. "It's him or your mother."

I looked at Mama, whose expression hadn't changed in,

well, in years. Nevertheless, I detected trace amounts of pathos.

"I suppose that's that, then," I said. "Sorry, Mama."

"Anty!"

"Now, be fair, you did actually murder someone," I pointed out. "My own father, if it's not putting too fine a point on it."

"I merely hastened the inevitable, Anthony," protested Mama. "It was a matter of a very short time before he stumbled in front of a tram entirely unprompted and unaided."

"No, I know," I sympathised. "I expect he left much to be desired as a life mate. And as a father, so long as we're speaking ill of the dead, but he was nevertheless dear old Papa. You know, I had dinner with him at his club only a few days before he disengaged the ignition. I clearly recall his last words to me, he said, 'Don't tell your mother about the barrel of brandy in the coal cellar,' and, until now, I've tried to live by those words."

"What the devil are you gassing on about, Boisjoly?" Deebee spoke anxiously. Doubtless his nerves, too, were affected by the storm.

"Please, Deebee, can't you see we're having a tender moment?" I admonished.

"Are you going to execute Thumpy or am I going to turn in your mother?"

"I'm thinking, Deebee," I dawdled. "Tell you what — I'll play you for it."

"What?"

"One hand, winner keeps the letter." I dealt us each one card up and one card down. He had a queen showing. I had a six.

Numbly and dumbly, like a red-sequined automaton, Deebee peaked at his face-down card. I turned mine up at the corner and gave Mama a sly smile.

Deebee's stunned stare rebounded between my simple, unassuming, baccarat face — unreadable, I'm told, because it could mean almost anything.

"Card," said Deebee. I dealt him a seven. He turned over a five for a total of two. I turned over a nine, for a total of five.

"Hard luck, Deebs," I said. "Well, Mama, it appears that you'll live to kill again."

"You stacked the deck," said Deebee, with surprising acuity for a killer.

"I did," I confessed. "I needed to do something to pass the time. Even then I had to tell you the entire tragedy of Drams Dewars' wedding song while everyone got into position."

"Position? Position for what?"

"The grand opening, Deebee."

Thunder rumbled in the distance. The rain continued in an unbroken shush. The room remained determinedly dark.

"I said," I repeated. "The grand opening, Deebee."

In the darkness was heard, "Op. One thousand sorries. I am the spoon," and the lights came on. Scattered applause came to us from the mezzanine, where the biddies, Jacqueline and Chaddy, Commodore Wairing, and The Astounding Bounding Bean stood at the railing. Rémy was behind the bar, and Roquebrune and Turbie were at the roulette and *vingt-et-un* tables.

"Of course." Deebee held up the letter. "It's fake."

"No, it's real enough," I said. "But Mama wrote it this afternoon, when we hatched this plan. You're right, Deebs, I couldn't prove that there were two Beanos or that you fired Malandrino out of a cannon into a cliff-face — who would ever believe that? — so I had to get you to admit to it in front of witnesses. And to do that, you needed to think that you had me where you wanted me — I believe it's called the formula."

CHAPTER TWENTY

Reconciliation
at the Riviera Royale

The following morning, Mama took me to the circus. I simultaneously learned that she had never been to a circus before, either.

"Why is that man up there, Anty?

We watched the spectacle from the bow deck of Little Miss Fortune under optimal weather for a water-borne circus. The storm, having fully expressed itself during the night, had withdrawn beyond the mountains to pout. A happy, hard-working sun snapped into action and cleaned things right up in the industrious way of a Mediterranean morning — none of that hazy hangover of your English storms. The sky was an unblemished canopy of an ornamental icing blue, and the sea a bouncy malachite mattress. There was no wind, as such, but rather a meandering, directionless wafting of maritime adventure and tropical flora and fish.

On either side of the beach, stacked stand seating had reached maximum occupancy of locals, drawn by Deebee's dubious handbills and ferried to the island by Little Miss Fortune's returning crew. The three rings of the beach circus were a chaos of jugglers and clowns and tumblers and a man breaking coconuts over his head. In the third and largest ring, a small brass band raced one another through *Entrance of the Gladiators,* and Thumpy trumpeted in whenever the spirit moved him. Above us, balanced on a cable held taut between the beach and the boat by an ingenious pulley mechanism, the Astounding Bounding Bean stood on one leg, playing an accordion.

"He's standing on one leg, Mama," I carefully explained, "playing an accordion."

"I can see that, Anty. What I asked was why."

"Ah, well, there you take me into deep waters, Sir Mumsalot. Perhaps the other leg is troubling him."

"Seems needlessly dangerous."

"I gather that's rather in the spirit of the thing," I reflected. "It's in the same sort of theme that the chap there, in the first ring, is setting fire to his expectorate, and the blindfolded bloke in the second ring is throwing knives at the underdressed girl on the rotating darts board."

"All this disarray is in deliberate aid of risking life and limb?" marvelled Mama. "I told you it was just like Piccadilly Circus."

"I concede the point."

"What is the fool doing now?"

"He appears to be diving into the water. Rather perilous, at that distance, I would have thought... ah, no, you see that? He's timed it to be swept up by that other chap on the trapeze."

"But now the oaf has let him go."

"I think that may have been planned — yes, there we are, the Bean has twirled for a bit and then latched onto a trapeze of his own. Seems an unlikely thing to happen by chance."

This mockery of the laws of physics and rules of common sense continued for some space of time. Meanwhile, we were joined by the biddies. Gone, now, were the mismatched sack dresses, yarn bags, and wilderness scene hats. The ladies wore sequinned swallowtail tuxedos — Mimpley in mauve, Biddicomb in blue — with matching top hats.

"What ho, fellow enthusiasts of neglected safety standards."

"Good morning, Anty, Cleo..." manifested Mimpley.

"...Riveting show, isn't it?" boosted Biddicomb.

"Isn't the Bounding Bean just so...

"...astounding?"

As this adulation unfolded, the Bean earned it by somersaulting free of his trapeze and landing neatly on the deck of the yacht. He held up his arms to receive and then dampen the applause, which was replaced by a drumroll. Beano donned a helmet and a parachute and then climbed a stepladder before the human-sized cannon. With a final wave, he fitted himself into the aperture. The drumroll increased its pace and the commodore appeared with an immense torch. The drum stopped, the commodore touched off the fuse, and with a small boom and an enormous puff of smoke, the Astounding Bounding Bean arced across the water like a tremendous lawn dart and disappeared into a bale of hay on the beach. The reaction of the audience was largely as expected, apart from Mama, who clapped her hands and let slip, "Oh, good show!"

"Mama."

"Yes, but Anty, did you see that? How is such a thing possible?"

"Just the right amount of gunpowder..." explained Mimpley.

"...and a thick plug of wadding," elucidated Biddicomb.

"And the right angle to achieve the trajectory," interpolated Mimpley.

"...it's simple ballistics," completed Biddicomb.

On the beach, the Bean rolled out of the haystack wearing judge's robes and juggling oversized gavels. Meanwhile, a jury of clowns opened Thumpy's cage and led him solemnly to the middle of the centre ring. A lone bugler played *The Last Post*.

Children in the crowd booed and pleaded for mercy as Beano armed himself with an oversized blunderbuss. He demanded order in his court. The bugler fell silent. Beano pointed the gun at Thumpy and pulled the trigger, producing a puff of confetti and a flag with 'BANG!' written on it. Thumpy, cooperating fully with his execution, rolled onto his back and kicked his feet in the air.

"What is to become of the elephant, Anty?" asked Mama.

"The very question that has been much on my mind," I

replied. "I have an idea, but it may require a small diversification of the Boisjoly investment portfolio, and a rather unprecedented degree of cooperation from our neighbours in Kensington."

"Oh, Thumpy's staying with the circus," said Mimpley.

"He and Beano work so well together, don't you think?" asked Biddicomb as Thumpy rolled back onto his feet to join Beano in a synchronised soft-shoe across the beach and back again.

"But, what about the circus itself?" I asked. "I can't imagine Deebee will be in a position to keep it going."

"Deebee sold the *Cirque d'Azur,* Mister Boisjoly..." said Mimpley.

"...to us," anticipated Biddicomb.

"Oh, right oh," I right-ohed. "All three rings?"

"He said that he had a much bigger opportunity," said Mimpley.

"In Monte Carlo," added Biddicomb.

"But, if it's not being indiscreet, was your money not tied up in the gambling syndicate?" I asked.

The biddies shared a shyly conspiratorial glance.

"We got our money back..."

"...with a profit of four thousand pounds."

"Well, that's jolly..." This promising thought was checked at the starting gate "...just a tic — when did all this come about?"

"Yesterday morning," synchronised the biddies.

A ripple of laughter and applause drew our collective attention back to the beach where Thumpy and the Bean were both dancing on rubber balls the size of a London taxi. Beano was attempting to juggle, of all things, watermelons, but was frustrated in his efforts by Thumpy, who would intermittently catch one and eat it. Thumpy's sense of comic timing, with the threat of the cat-o-nine-tails removed from the equation, was positively Chaplinesque.

"All set, ladies." The commodore, looking fully oceangoing

in a white admiral's jacket and cap, clipped up with a smart salute.

"What ho, Commodore," I said. "You're looking very very dairy."

"Like it?" The commodore posed nautically. "It's actually a head waiter's uniform. I won it off Rémy last night at Brooms."

"Most becoming," I assured him. "Your luck's taken a turn for the better."

"Could hardly be much worse, could it? But, yes, the docket's paid, the crew's come back, not so sure luck has much to do with it." The commodore expressed this happy notion in a heel-clicking bow to the biddies.

"It may be related," I suggested. "It was Malandrino who worked out your arrangement with Deebee, was it not?"

"Yes, that's right."

"And it was Deebee who negotiated your concession agreements with the hotels and casinos who, for one reason or another, were never able to pay."

"Yes, that's... oh, right, yes, I see what you mean." The commodore nodded sagely. "You think that Deebee was bad luck."

"Near enough."

"Coming ashore for the finale, Boisjolys?" asked the commodore.

"We both feel that this is a spectacle best observed from a distance." Mama studied Thumpy who, at that moment, was playing a sort of jumbo cricket, striking watermelons with an immense bat. "Yours is a brave new world."

I watched the biddies and commodore putter ashore but Mama gazed towards the point.

"They're not coming, Mama," I said.

"Doubtless Jacqueline is still in bed. It's not even noon."

Mama spoke without conviction. She never speaks with conviction, but her tone on this occasion carried less emotive sincerity it does when she says 'Thank you, Vickers.'

"I expect they're in Monte Carlo already." I mentally ordered the events to this moment; the steamer trunk recovered by Pilque with all of Malandrino's worldly possessions, Jacqueline assuring me that the clown had shuffled off his mortal mouse ears before she could cheat any money out of him, the biddies receiving four thousand pounds yesterday morning, then Deebee telling me that I'd been sold out for that exact amount, and then me standing on the deck of a yacht watching an elephant explode watermelons with a cricket bat and, amazingly, finding almost no humour in it. Jacqueline and Chadwick helped the biddies buy their circus, they helped me help Thumpy, and then they helped themselves.

"I'm sorry, Anty." Perhaps it was the wind or the hush of the sea but it sounded subtly and fleetingly as though, this time, Mama had spoken with conviction.

"No matter. Heartbreak, happily, has a neat remedy. It can also be taken with ice or seltzer." I looked away from the beach, where the biddies were accepting a bouquet of flowers from Thumpy, towards the point where vain hope dissolved on empty waters. "In any case, as you've pointed out, I was raised with the emotional depth of a circus mogul. Doubtless I'll fall in love with someone equally or more hopelessly unattainable on the boat home."

"Must you go back straight away?"

"I thought I might linger on a bit, in point of fact." I abandoned coast guard duty and returned my attention to Mama. "Still haven't tried the Riviera Royale's famous Collage Pie."

"That would be most welcome." Mama directed her words to the beach. "I could teach you to play baccarat."

"I know how to play baccarat."

"No, Anty, you know the rules to baccarat. There's little point in playing if you don't win."

"Papa, on the other hand, always used to say 'there's no point in playing if you're unlikely to end up in the papers.' Is it any wonder I turned out so capricious with all these mixed messages?"

"These are valuable life lessons."

"Of course they are," I agreed. "Just not for any life you or I have ever known. I recall you once telling me that it was vital to be ruthless with every opponent."

"I was teaching you about life."

"You were teaching me whist."

"At least you learned to keep an eye on your trumps."

"A lesson I'm unlikely to quickly forget," I said. "Took me a week to win back Mister Snaardvark."

Mama regarded me from the edge of a surreptitious squint.

"You know, Anty, I was very impressed with how you resolved everything so cleverly."

"I can hardly take all the credit," I demurred. "Without your native dishonesty and Aunt Jacqueline's flare for fraud, it might easily have taken me till later this afternoon to put Deebee in the frame."

"It's not only that to which I refer, Anty." Mama afforded me another half an eye. "Of course I read about your triumph in Fray. It was in all the papers. And your aunt Azalea and I have been in regular correspondence since you sorted out that business at Christmas. I've been following your activities scrupulously, but I couldn't say so when you arrived. I could hardly have it said that I was boasting about my son."

"No one would ever accuse you of that."

"I'm sorry I misled you, Anty."

"Frankly, Mama, it's more surprising that you're finally telling the truth."

"There's no call for sarcasm, Anty."

"It's how I navigate awkward moments," I said, "and genial occasions and chance encounters, for that matter. I think it's an involuntary reflex. Am I doing it now? I can't even tell."

"I want you to know that I'm proud of you, Anty."

"Oh yes? Well, a Boisjoly can give as good as he gets," I countered. "I'm proud of you, too, Mumps. You handled yourself with Deebee like a seasoned professional. One would think you'd been confessing to murders your whole life."

"Obviously it's been much on my mind since your father's funeral."

"Has it?" This put me a bit off-balance, I don't mind saying. "Might one enquire why?"

Now Mama turned her attention fully to me, in the manner of one sharing a delicate confidence or an off-colour limerick. "I was ready to admit to everything, if it proved necessary."

"If it proved necessary?"

"Obviously, I always hoped it wouldn't." Mama glanced around the empty deck. "But I'm prepared to take full responsibility."

I wasn't sure what I'd been planning or hoping for this moment. Probably that it would simply never come. "Very well, Mama. I suppose we'd best finally have this reckoning — did you arrange to pop off Papa?"

"I beg your pardon." Mama stepped back and, without moving a facial muscle, somehow expressed that uneasy blend of bewilderment and dismay that I see so often. "Of course not. I thought you did."

"You thought I hired someone to push Papa under an electric tram?"

"Well, it was all so suspicious," said Mama, "everything happening so suddenly, just after your father changed his will in your favour."

"I was unaware of that," I pointed out austerely. "If anyone behaved suspiciously, it was you."

"How so?"

"You left right after the funeral," I said. "Actually, you left during the funeral. You missed the quiz round."

"I had a train."

"And it was you who hired a professional assassin as Papa's private secretary."

"Who said she was a professional assassin? She was the simple-minded daughter of the chap who did the gutters. Writes for the Society page of the Times, now, I believe."

"Vickers recognised her," I said.

193

"Vickers? You're placing your faith in something that Vickers observed since 1911?"

"Yes, fair point," I conceded. "But you'll admit you pulled strings to nobble the inquest."

"Of course."

"But this only drew suspicion to you," I noted.

"Well, obviously, Anty, that was the deliberate point of the exercise."

"But, why?"

"What do you mean, why?"

"I mean, quite evidently in my view, why would you want the chattering classes to think that you had been responsible for the precipitous lowering of Papa's body temperature?"

"So that they wouldn't think that you were." Mama spoke with her Professor of the Plainly Obvious tone, the one she would use when outlining in simple terms the complex class structure which, whether we like it or no, means that five-year-old boys do not marry their governesses. "I blocked the inquest so that it wouldn't turn up something that might incriminate you."

"Do I understand you to say that you believed that there was a chance that I was responsible for Papa's early doors?"

"You thought I'd done it."

"That's true," I said. "Well, then, why were you prepared to confess to it?"

"Anthony," A single eyebrow escaped the confines of Mama's sequestered features, "I'm your mother."

On the beach a parade had been assembled and it was doing a sort of victory lap, interacting with children, accepting peanuts and accolades, and providing Thumpy new scope for artistic expression. The sun clocked into position dutifully overhead and, accompanied by a puff of smoke over the water, the midday cannon faithfully fired.

Anty Boisjoly Mysteries

Thank you for reading *Reckoning at the Riviera Royale,* the fifth Anty Boisjoly mystery. I very much hope that you enjoyed it. I certainly enjoyed writing it and finally introducing Anty's mom and revealing a bit more of his history. I also think *Reckoning at the Riviera Royale* included one of the more original impossible murders that Anty has had to untangle and I hope you didn't see it coming.

If you liked this story and whether or not you were able to figure out some or most of the mystery, I hope you'll tell your friends about *Reckoning on the Riviera Royale.*

Now I think of it, if your friends don't already know about *Reckoning at the Riviera Royale,* then they probably don't know about the rest of Anty Boisjoly's mysteries, so here's a handy guide:

The Case of the Canterfell Codicil

The first Anty Boisjoly mystery

In The Case of the Canterfell Codicil, Wodehousian gadabout and clubman Anty Boisjoly takes on his first case when his old Oxford chum and coxswain is facing the gallows, accused of the murder of his wealthy uncle. Not one but two locked-room mysteries later, Boisjoly's pitting his wits and witticisms against a subversive butler, a senile footman, a single-minded detective-inspector, an irascible goat, and the eccentric conventions of the pastoral Sussex countryside to untangle a multi-layered mystery of secret bequests, ancient writs, love triangles, revenge, and a teasing twist in the final paragraph.

The Case of the Ghost of Christmas Morning

The Christmas number

In The Case of the Ghost of Christmas Morning, clubman, flaneur, idler and sleuth Anty Boisjoly pits his sardonic wits against another pair of impossible murders. This time, Anty Boisjoly's Aunty Boisjoly is the only possible suspect when a murder victim stands his old friends a farewell drink at the local, hours after being murdered.

The Tale of the Tenpenny Tontine

The dual duel dilemma

It's another mystifying, manor house murder for bon-vivant and problem-solver Anty Boisjoly, when his clubmate asks him to determine who died first after a duel is fought in a locked room. The untold riches of the Tenpenny Tontine are in the balance, but the stakes only get higher when Anty determines that, duel or not, this was a case of murder.

The Case of the Carnaby Castle Curse

The scary one

The ancient curse of Carnaby Castle has begun taking victims again — either that, or someone's very cleverly done away with the new young bride of the philandering family patriarch, and the chief suspect is none other than Carnaby, London's finest club steward.

Anty Boisjoly's wits and witticisms are tested to their frozen limit as he sifts the superstitions, suspicions, and age-old schisms of the mediaeval Peak District village of Hoy to sort out how it was done before the curse can claim Carnaby himself.

Reckoning at the Riviera Royale

The one with Anty's mum

Anty finally has that awkward 'did you murder my father' conversation with his mother while finding himself in the ticklish position of defending her and an innocent elephant against charges of impossible murder.

The Next Anty Boisjoly Mystery

There's always a new Anty Boisjoly mystery in the offing, and if you'd like to be kept current to his gadding about, you can sign up for early-bird announcements...

https://indefensiblepublishing.com/books/pj-fitzsimmons/

Ingram Content Group UK Ltd.
Milton Keynes UK
UKHW011307010523
421052UK00004B/291

9 782958 039257